Modern

Persuasion

21ST CENTURY AUSTEN 1

SARA MARKS

ILLUMINATED MYTH PUBLISHING

Illuminated Myth Publishing

https://www.illuminatedmyth.com/

Fourth Edition – March 2022

http://saramarks.net

Print ISBN-13: 978-1545527832

Cover Design by 100 Covers

https://100covers.com/

To Grammy and Nana, I wish you had both been here to see this happen.
To Anita and Frank, who may have had their own plans for my life, but always support the ones I make on my own.

Also By

The 21ˢᵗ Century Austen Series

MODERN PERSUASION

Unraveling Carrie Woodhouse (#5)

The Yom Tov Romance Series
Purim Fling
Matzo Ball Billionaire
Forgive Me, I Love You
Latkes of Love

Anthologies
"Open to Negotiations" in Dangerous Curves Ahead
"The Prince Without A Throne" in Wickedly Ever After

Chapter One

"Y our father's art collection is quite... large," said the woman sitting before me.

She was in her mid-sixties with a jet black pixie haircut and glasses with thick black frames. She wore a fitted black suit and carried a black leather portfolio as she walked around the apartment. She had been part of the New York art scene for most of her life and had been recommended to me by most of the people I spoke to.

We were sitting on wooden boxes in the Upper East-side NYC apartment that has been in my father's family since, in his words only, the dawn of time. This woman was trying to pick her words carefully. To be fair, the fact that we could sit anywhere in this apartment surprised me. My father's art collection was a hoard. This woman knew perfectly well that inside the box on which she sat was some piece of art he was refusing to part with. I was sitting on another box. I knew what this woman would tell me next.

1

She was here to tell my father the reality of the situation. The only problem was that my father was not in the room to hear it. He was off explaining his selection criteria to my older sister. He believed this woman and I were with them.

"You can be honest. I know he hasn't purchased items of value," I said in an attempt to speed this up.

She didn't make eye contact with me as she wrote something on her pad. "Well, to be fair, he has picked items from important artists."

"Yes, but he doesn't pick valuable items and pays more than they're worth," I said, letting my shoulders sag.

"Yes, you're correct," she finally looked up and gave me an encouraging smile.

I shook my head. "I've told him this for years."

"Walter seems to have some type of criteria for selection, though," she said and closed her portfolio. "I'm unclear how he makes such bad choices."

I could hear my father continuing to talk about that very criterion in another room. While a spoiled brat, my sister would allow him to continue to share the justifications he had developed over our lifetimes.

I leaned to the side to look down the hall, ensuring he wasn't coming. "I love my father, but he's full of shit," I said, lowering my voice. "His real criteria is to buy pieces by anyone people are talking about, but to pick the pieces that... well, he probably just picks the first one he sees."

"You can make money selling these pieces," the woman said, raising an eyebrow.

"Just not enough to make up for what he paid," I said, holding up a finger.

She nodded and sighed. "Yes."

"Can you lie to him?"

"How so?" she asked, raising an eyebrow.

I glanced down the hall one more time. "Tell him he can make money selling all these pieces. He needs the money much more than he needs art, even if he doesn't make enough money."

"Fine," she said with a sigh.

I was exhausted by the time the appraiser left. I had wasted a lovely spring Saturday in New York City dealing with my father, Elizabeth, and the art hoard. I wanted to go home, drink an entire bottle of wine, and fall asleep while reading manuscripts for work. I couldn't, as I had to supervise the movers who were boxing up the art.

"Emma, you're breaking my heart," my father said after the appraiser left.

He slumped on one of the large boxes and picked at the corner of a piece of tape.

I felt terrible, understanding that I was unraveling his world. "Someone has to make the difficult decisions."

He waved an arm toward my sister's room. "Next, you're going to make Elizabeth sell her shoes."

I winced. "She's going to have to do that too. You can sell the apartment, or you can sell the stuff. The decision is yours."

"Emma," he said, straightening up, "this apartment has been in our family since the dawn of time."

He may have been exaggerating, but my family had been living in the apartment for generations. It wasn't large, but it had once fit five people with a little room to spare.

My father had filled the space with art over the last ten years. Every inch of wall space was taken up by abstract and modern paintings. Every flat surface had a sculpture on it. Even the bathrooms had been filled with some type of art.

My sister Elizabeth, who still lived in the room the three of us had shared as children, allowed my father's art to invade her space. That is, what space was not already filled with her crates of designer shoes and purses. She had them stacked up along a wall with labels of what was inside each container. At least Elizabeth was organized, but items were never taken out of their crates after the first use. She still hadn't noticed that I often took purses and shoes from her collection, even when she saw the shoes on my feet and the purse in my hands.

"Then the art has to go. You need the money to live on," I said, putting my hand on his shoulder.

"If I sell the art, can we stay in the apartment?" my father asked, his voice wavering slightly.

I shook my head, frowning. "No, you can rent something less expensive in Westchester and use the rent from this apartment to support yourself. You have gone through almost all of your retirement money because of the art."

I could see the tears begin to fill his eyes. "Art's important. Who would you be if you had not grown up surrounded by my art?"

"There is a difference between your art collection before Mom's death and now," I said as I sat down next to him and put an arm over his shoulders. "I would've been fine with you showing restraint or picking valuable pieces that we could sell for more than you bought them for."

"Time will tell on their value," my father whispered.

I put my head on my father's shoulder. "You don't have time. You need money now."

"What about my shoes?" My older sister Elizabeth said, coming into the room.

I stood up, having far less sympathy for Elizabeth's situation than I did for our father. "You need money too. Get a job or sell the shoes. While you are at it, sell some of your purses and clothes. Also, get a job. You've blown through the money Mom left you when she passed."

They didn't get it and probably never would. I couldn't leave until the apartment was empty, so I stayed another few hours. Art was packed and moved to the auction house while the remaining items were sent to the rented townhouse in Westchester. My younger sister Mary was on that end waiting to receive the moving trucks and let the movers into the house. My father and Elizabeth had rented a car and took their personal items to get settled quickly. I was left to supervise the cleaning crew and get the apartment ready for new tenants. I left the key with the concierge before I left the building and followed everyone to Westchester to supervise the bookend of this adventure. I was barely out of the building parking lot when my phone rang.

"The truck is here," Mary said before I could even say hello.

"Great. Get them unpacking," I said, navigating the city traffic.

"Emma, I am not feeling great. I really need to go home and relax. Plus, the boys need dinner. How long before you get here?" My younger sister said with a whine that was part of her natural speaking voice.

I massaged my temple as I waited at a light. "I'm not even out of the city yet. I just got into the car. It'll be at least an hour."

"Can't you drive faster?" she said in a whisper.

I suspected she was trying to remain unheard.

"It's not a matter of faster," I said as the light changed and I needed to focus again. "Just deal with things, and you can leave when I get there."

"Are you staying with me?" She asked, her voice getting louder since she would want to make sure Elizabeth heard which of my sisters I preferred.

I was too focused on the road to push back. "I was hoping to if it's ok with you."

"Of course it is. I set up the spare room. The boys are terribly excited that you are staying with us."

"I'm staying through Sunday," I reminded her. "I can take Louisa with me into the city for work on Monday. I'll spend more time with you and the boys once we are on Cape Cod for vacation."

"Louisa's very excited. She can't wait to tell you about her first week," Mary added, now perky as we talked about her life.

"Ok, can I focus on driving then?" I said as I stopped for some people randomly crossing the street. "I promise it won't be more than another hour at the most."

"Fine, but I really need you here. Dad and Elizabeth are just ignoring me."

I wasn't surprised since this had been the case nearly all of Mary's life.

"Just deal with the movers. Dad and Elizabeth are just irritated with the whole situation," I said before hanging up and putting on some music for the rest of my drive.

As much as I love my family, I resent them more than I probably should. Not that I would ever let them know that.

The drive had been easy once I had gotten out of the city. I arrived at the townhouse thirty-five minutes later. Even though it was dark out, I could clearly see my sister Mary directing the movers as they carried things into the house.

"That was the last box!" Mary said when she saw me get out of my car.

I gave her a hug, grateful that she had managed it all without needing to call me. "You did that faster than I expected."

"Once I got Dad and Elizabeth out of the way, it was a breeze," she said, glowing under the praise.

"Are they unpacking?" I asked as we started walking toward the door.

Mary sighed and shook her head. "He's complaining about the art he had to sell. She's in her room, making sure her stuff's undamaged. They aren't going to make any changes, are they?"

I gave her a small smile, glad I could count on her to be rational and to back me up. "It's doubtful. They both seem to think I've been secretly hoarding his money for such a situation."

"You set up the trust with what's left, right?" Mary asked with a look of panic on her face. "I mean, there's some left, right?"

When she passed away, my mother left her small fortune to my sisters and me. While we all used it to pay for college, we spent the remaining money in different ways. Mary followed our mother's example and put her share away in various accounts and trusts so her children could have it someday. Elizabeth spent hers on shoes, purses, and clothes. I used mine to buy an apartment in the city. My father had his own money and a retirement account he had blown through while buying his art.

In the ten years since our mother died, we had taken on atypical roles for our place in age order. Instead of being the responsible, practical, older child, Elizabeth had never been denied anything or expected to make anything of her life. My father was happy to still have her living with him at home. She had no responsibilities beyond her own imagined ones. Mary, the youngest, turned into an attention-seeking middle child. That left me in the middle, acting as the responsible and practical one. Mary had her own family to take care of, so I had allowed myself to take on the burden of paternal care.

"Yes, the rent from the apartment will be used to pay the rent and bills here," I said, ticking items off my fingers. "The credit cards have been canceled and are being paid off with the money from the art auction. It won't bring in enough, but they're getting an allowance. If either of them gets a new credit card, then I wash my hands of this once and for all."

Later, I got to Mary's house to find it filled with people, food, and wine. Mary's in-laws, the Musgroves, filled the house with good cheer. It was completely different from the world we had grown up in. I understood why my younger sister found herself drawn to her husband's family over her own. Mary's attention-seeking nature can be annoying. The Musgrove family give my sister the attention she needs and I love that about them. They adore her and her children, and she is far less annoying because they give her so much attention. I enjoy her much more now than I did as a child, even though I always liked her more than Elizabeth. I was fourteen when my mother passed away. Elizabeth was sixteen, and Mary was eleven. Our mother had been the anchor of the family. She kept my father from spending all their money and building the art hoard that would grow once she passed. They were always restrained, and showing affection was rare. They weren't uptight but products of their social class.

It was nice to spend time with the Musgroves. I could relax a bit when I was around this family. They were boisterous and loving. I had gotten their youngest, Louisa, a summer internship at my publishing house. She was clearly anxious to tell me about her first week since the entire company was getting ready to go to PubCon next week. PubCon was the largest publishing conference in North America. Publishers from all over the U.S., Canada, and worldwide came to show their newest titles, meet with new authors, and share with booksellers and librarians. My father's family had owned a publishing company for generations, so I had been going to PubCon since birth. My father allowed his company to be purchased by a larger one and had run the imprint until his retirement. He and my mother had met as young editors early in their careers. My mother's best friend, and my mentor, Karen Russell, had been hired by my parents, and she eventually hired me. I believed Karen's plan was to have me run the entire company one day. As a result of growing up in the publishing industry, going to PubCon each year didn't have the same excitement for me as it did for Louisa.

"So, I've been assigned to work with one of our new authors," Louisa told me after a late dinner in a conspiratorial whisper.

"Who?" Mary asked from across the room.

My younger sister hated to be left out of any conversation and could hear across rooms if she felt she was being left out.

"You know that screenwriter..." Louisa said, waving her hand. "Oh, I can't remember his name. You'll remember,

Mary. He wrote that movie about that guy who dated an actress, and she left him for someone better. Then, last year, it really happened to him."

"Oh, Fredrick Wentworth!" Mary said, perking up.

Chapter Two

F redrick Wentworth, Fred as I remembered him (and Freddy, as only I was allowed to call him), was the last name I expected to hear Louisa say. I'm not sure why. I knew he was publishing a book and that we were his publishers. Karen had turned down the chance to have our team work with him. To be fair, she probably turned it down because of my history with him.

When my mother passed away, Karen stepped in to help my father raise his three teenage daughters. Elizabeth was clearly my father's favorite, even when my mother was alive. Karen felt sorry for Mary and me, but it was clear that she favored me. Karen thought she was teaching me to see the world the way my mother would have wanted.

As a product of her generation, Karen considers herself a feminist. She's an advocate for women in the workplace, equal pay, ending rape culture, and all of that stuff. She taught me that I couldn't have it all, no matter what the

13

media told me. Instead, I learned how to pick what was most important to me; confident Karen was an example of a woman who chose her priorities well. She opted not to marry and have children because she wanted her career. She was happy to live through her friends and their families. At twenty-two, when I graduated from college, she persuaded me that I had to make the same choice she did. I was in love with a man who wanted a life in Los Angeles, but I wanted to work in an industry that existed almost exclusively in New York City. To make the decision even more stressful, I had already taken on the mantle of caring for my father.

I met Fredrick, then Fred, the summer before my junior year at Northwestern University in Chicago. A friend and I had decided to rent an apartment together off-campus instead of sharing a dorm room. We found a great furnished apartment close to campus. Then said friend fell in love and left me alone to move in with her new boyfriend. Fredrick took over the lease. Fredrick was a tall, slender man at six-foot-four inches, with dark-reddish blond hair, brown eyes, and awkwardness that was really cute. He still had some baby fat that rounded his oval face when we met, but his smile was wide and happy. We started dating in the middle of the summer, and we stayed together until graduation.

I remember graduation so clearly. My father and Karen came to celebrate with me. Since my father doesn't like anyone from outside his social circle, I had no expectation that he would approve of Fredrick, but I didn't care. It was only Karen's opinion that mattered. Fredrick had proposed to me just before graduation. I had not given him an answer, anxious about what would change in my life if I accepted. When I confided in her, Karen was positive that Fredrick was the wrong guy for me. I remember her list of reasons very well.

- He wants you to move to LA.
- You know nobody in LA.
- There are no publishing companies in LA (of importance).
- Your entire family is in NYC.
- You will reduce your entire identity to just being a wife and mother instead of a complex and important woman.

I remember my list of reasons to marry him just as well.

- I love him, and he makes me happy.

Rationality won over love. Karen listed three questions when I told her my reason to marry him:

- How happy would I be if I was lonely and bored in LA?
- How quickly would I resent him if I was unhappy?
- How much longer would I love him if I resented him?

I rejected his proposal, ended the relationship, moved back to NYC, and assured myself that I would soon meet someone. The only problem was that I never did. Oh, I dated, but I never met anyone who made me feel the way Fredrick made me feel. Karen didn't consult me when she turned down the chance to work with Fredrick, but I understood why.

I tried to ignore stories about Fredrick after the breakup eight years ago, but it proved impossible to do that. Three years after we broke up, he wrote a hit movie about it. I didn't realize he was the screenwriter until I saw his name on the opening credits. Friends dragged me to the theatre, swearing it was funny, cute, and the girlfriend was a bitch. The movie focused on a man who proposed to his actress girlfriend only to be rejected. The girlfriend left him to be with someone famous. The man finds out his life is better without the ex-girlfriend and rejects her in exchange when she begs his forgiveness. In tears, I left the movie early because it took me all of one minute to realize I was the inspiration for the girlfriend. She may not have been named Emma or looked like me, but this movie must be the story of what Fredrick wished happened after our breakup. I kept all of this to myself and insisted to my friends that I walked out because I hate romantic comedies.

After that, it was impossible to avoid news of Fred, now known as Fredrick. He was everywhere in popular culture. He dated a string of famous actresses, wrote popular television shows and movies, started producing popular television shows and movies, and more. Then, about six months ago, the press coverage got excessive after proposing to his current girlfriend (coincidently a struggling actress). As if in a movie, she turned Fredrick down and started dating a very famous actor, soon after married him, and was already getting divorced. People thought his hit movie had become reality, and the press couldn't get enough of the parallels. That's when he decided to write a book for middle school boys. It was due to come out in two days.

Chapter Three

Early in the morning, I met Louisa outside the Javits Center. It was the first day of PubCon, and she was anxious about what to expect. I had seen plenty of people get overwhelmed by just the building alone. It took up six city blocks. Inside it was three and a half floors primarily of open space for conventions. It was challenging to find the right place to be, and the lines of attendees were already forming at the exhibit floor entrances. Sometimes two or three events were going on at once. I had even attended graduations here.

After much whining and cajoling, Mary convinced me to buy her a ticket to PubCon too. Her plan was to walk around aimlessly, getting free books from the publishers. I used the opportunity to get her to pick up books for me. Mary, like me, had been going to PubCon most of her life. We had grown up in a family of publishers and readers. My father's book collection was technically smaller than his art collection. That's because he has actual knowledge of what's valuable with books, so he's more selective with that collection. When Mary and I had first talked about raising money, we quickly nixed the idea of selling his books. We both had memories of those books being read to us at night and learning to read using them. At PubCon, we always went through the books we picked up and bet on what would be the most successful. Mary had a knack for knowing which book would sell the best, but I knew which would get the awards.

Working in the publishing industry meant that I was at PubCon as a professional, so I didn't have much time to walk around. I had appointments almost all day. The first day was critical because I had two authors doing signing events at our booth. One author was new and had no idea what to expect. The other was a publishing veteran and a popular draw to our booth. While she didn't actually work with me, Louisa spent most of the first day following me around.

"This is insane!" Louisa said, her mouth agape, as we walked into the Javits Center. "Is it always like this?"

There were people everywhere. Louisa was dressed like a party in ugly high heels, a cute dress, and full makeup. I had told her to dress comfortably but professionally. Her choice of shoes was always a problem. I, meanwhile, wore jeans, boots, and a blouse. I didn't have to spend my day staffing the booth, but Louisa was going to be on her feet the entire day. I expected her to complain after a few hours.

I focused on the crowds while Louisa looked around at the banners hanging from the rafters, all advertising the major releases being featured. "These are librarians, authors, agents, and publishers," I said, holding on to her wrist so we didn't get separated. "They don't get too crazy. Security is at the entrances to ensure everyone has a badge to get in. You don't have to worry about a mob at the booth. These people know how to queue for autographing."

Our badges allowed us to enter the exhibit hall ahead of the crowd and the security guard waved us through when she saw the bright orange stripe on our name badges. I let go of Louisa's hand as we walked together through the empty exhibit floor.

"This place will be a zoo in about thirty minutes when it opens," I said as we got to the quiet booth, and I showed Louisa where to stash her things. "Your job is to stay there, handing people books, managing lines, and all of that. There is someone who will tell you what to do and when."

Louisa looked around, still in awe of the booth our company had set up. "Am I going to have free time to walk around?" Louisa asked without looking down at me.

I shrugged, looking to see who was around. "I don't know, but don't expect it."

"Will you be at the booth?" Louisa asked, finally looking at me with a bright smile.

I suspected she had heard Mary's stories of what it was like when we were children and wanted to have a friend to hang out with. I smiled, wishing I had at least a few hours to give to her today. "Only when my authors are signing. If you need me, I will be in our meeting areas," I said and squeezed her arm.

Louise leaned closer and whispered. "Who are you meeting?"

"Authors and agents," I said with a slight chuckle.

"Why can't I do that too?"

I shook my head. "You're an intern, not an editor. Your job is to work at the booth."

Louise pouted. "Oh. Well, maybe someday then."

Neither of us knew at the time how quickly her role would shift.

I should have paid more attention to the booth schedule, but I was only interested in my authors. I was pleased at the end of the first day. My new author had generated quite a bit of attention and interest. The line had been steady through her signing, and she didn't seem worn out. My veteran author was a powerhouse with a line wrapping around the exhibit floor. I'd asked the booth staff to manage the line with a ticket system so that people didn't wait needlessly. It was a good call since there weren't enough books for those who wanted them. It was good that we were giving away un-autographed copies the next day. This was a test of one way to manage the giveaways that could quickly get out of hand. We expected a crowd on the last day when the general public could attend. This was the first time the conference organizers were allowing this. None of us knew what to expect.

"So, you signed a new author?" Mary asked over dinner later that night.

Louisa had bowed out of dinner because her feet were so blistered from standing in heels all day. Mary and I ended up at a small and busy Italian restaurant in Midtown by my apartment.

I leaned into the table, closer to my sister, to share this news. "Yes, what's interesting is that her agent specifically wants her to work with me. He actually wants it written into her contract that if I leave, then she can leave with me."

Mary leaned closer and kept her voice as low as possible. "Is that a thing?"

"I have no idea," I said with a shrug, "I've never had anyone ask for it before."

Mary blinked a few times as she processed this. "Are you looking for a new job?"

"No," I said as I rapidly shook my head.

"Has this agent worked with you before?"

"Nope."

"That's weird," Mary said before leaning back and taking a bite of her salad.

"He wasn't the only one who requested it, either," I added before sitting back. "He's just the one with an author that I think has potential to have a great book."

"It doesn't really surprise me that people want to work with you," Mary said, giving me a wink. "You work with what, ten authors regularly?"

"There are about fifteen on my plate, but only ten really need any attention," I said, turning my hand a few times.

"Right," Mary added, stabbing some lettuce with a fork, "all ten of those are popular authors who regularly appear on bestseller lists and win awards. From what I saw today, your newest author is another win for you. You know how to pick books and get them to readers. From what I remember when Daddy ran the publishing house, I am surprised you don't get a ton of offers to work for other publishers."

Mary didn't know how right she was. Part of the reason I didn't wander around PubCon was that I often got stopped by publishers and offered jobs. I had never considered changing anything about my job.

Chapter Four

I arrived alone and early at PubCon on the second day.
I had been thinking about my dinner with Mary since
I got home, and my walk to Javits Center didn't help
clear my head. I had always trusted Karen to steer my
career in the right direction and never regretted it. She
had mentored me for the first few years, and I was quickly
promoted to editor. Karen remained the Executive Editor supervising me. While I was free to pick authors and
books to work with, she could veto my decisions. These
weird requests from agents and authors to add me to their
contracts were not something I had ever been asked to do
before. I couldn't help but dwell on what I was missing.

It was true that my career had slowed as my father's
finances had diminished. That sucked up so much of my
time and energy. I had nothing left for office politics and
to fight for myself. Karen knew what I was dealing with
because she was one of the two people trying to support

me - the other being Mary. I promised myself that, now that my father and Elizabeth's situation was better, I would use PubCon to shift my focus back on fighting for the career I wanted. If these editors wanted to work directly with me, I would fight to make sure that happened. I needed to make sure I was paying attention to the political games. This week was always when interesting shifts happened.

As I walked into the quiet convention center, I put that out of my mind. I was here early for a ticketed breakfast that I had been invited to attend by one of the authors on the panel, Tom Scott. My father had once been his publisher, and even though Tom changed publishers years later, they remained friends. He was the biggest draw to this breakfast, and his new book was prominently displayed around the open areas. I planned to stay just long enough to hear him speak. My VIP status allowed me to go backstage early, where I found him reading over his notes.

"Emma, sweetheart!" Tom said, getting to his feet to hug me.

"The line is so long it has doubled on itself," I said, letting him give me one of his long, comforting hugs like he had done when I was a kid. "They're finally letting everyone take their seats."

"Yes," he said when he let me go, and we sat down again. "This breakfast has a lot of attention. Some popular books and authors are included."

I looked around, surprised that he was the only one here so soon before they were going to take their spots. It gave me a moment to assess how Tom looked and adjust a few details. He was a tall, rail-thin man with jet black hair and a long oval face. He usually wore bifocals, but the lack of line across his glasses lenses made it clear he had finally upgraded his eyewear. He was dressed in baggy, stonewashed jeans that I was sure he had purchased around the time I was born but held up with black suspenders over a bright white button-down shirt with a pocket on each breast.

"Thank you for making me one of your VIPs," I said, happy to have this time alone with him.

Tom folded up his notes and put the paper in his front shirt pocket. "Well, I wanted to talk to you about that, first," he said and looked around to make sure we were alone before lowering his voice. "This is my last book under my contract. I'm considering a new publisher, and I want to work with you, no matter what company you work for. Are you up for it?"

I stared at him and blinked a few times. I wasn't sure what to make of that comment. "What?" I asked, doing my best to regain my composure. "Why would you switch publishers, and why might my position be in question?"

Tom tilted his head to the side and looked at me before smiling. "Personal reasons, and you have become the hottest editor. Everyone wants to work with you. There are rumors."

"Rumors?" I asked, narrowing my eyes.

Tom turned his head and looked around. I turned to look in the same direction and noticed people were beginning to enter. "I hear that you are going to start your own imprint, that you are switching jobs, that you are getting promoted, that you're taking back your family's publishing company and tons of others. All the talk is about you," he said, leaning close and whispering to me.

The requests from authors and agents were starting to make sense. I was sure these rumors were making people anxious, but I had no idea what had prompted them. I opened my mouth to assure him this was just gossip until I heard my name.

"OMG! Emma!" Someone called out from the other side of the room.

I looked up and saw Louisa waving to me. Standing next to her was Fredrick Wentworth with a look of complete shock on his face.

I don't know how much time passed once I met Fredrick's eyes. It seemed like he and Louisa walked towards me in slow motion. I could see Tom stand up and extend his hand to Louisa and Fredrick from the corner of my eye. My mind yelled at me to introduce Tom and to act like I was meeting Fredrick for the first time. I managed to get to my feet, but it felt like someone had punched me in the gut, and I was focused simply on breathing. Fortunately, Louisa kept talking as if nobody else had something to say.

"So, we were standing here getting ready, and Freddy... Can I call you Freddy? So, Freddy asks who is talking to Tom Scott. I mean, right, who is so important that she gets to talk to TOM SCOTT! And I was all like, that's my sister-in-law EMMA! You know Tom Scott? I mean, WOW! That is, like, huge, and Tom Scott is like the most important author in the world. I knew I just had to introduce you to Freddy, but also so I could introduce Freddy to Tom Scott. You know, so I could also meet Tom Scott. It is like a total honor to meet you, sir," Louisa continued on as Fredrick Wentworth and I stared at each other.

Even after all this time, I could still read Fredrick. The shock faded from his face as he worked through the logic of why I was here. I wondered if he had even considered me when picking a publisher for his book. I watched as he cringed and realized he hadn't even thought about where I would be working. He had given no thought to me when he entered the world I left him to be part of.

Fredrick was the panel moderator, and Tom was the first speaker. I really didn't want to sit through anything Fredrick Wentworth had to say. I had seen the movie, so I knew what he thought of me, and I didn't need to hear more. Still, I owed Tom my time and attention since he had used one of his three passes to invite me.

The ample space was filled with people. At the front of the room was a stage where the five featured authors sat at a long table in speaking order. That put Fredrick and Tom right next to each other over breakfast. Next were the tables where guests of the authors and those willing to pay for the expensive tickets sat. We got a higher quality breakfast - basically, more than muffins. Behind us was another group of tables. These people paid to only get muffins. The back of the space, taking up more than half of the audience, were the rows of chairs. These were the least expensive tickets, and there was no food for them. Most brought something in from the many restaurants serving breakfast. Food might not have been an option for everyone, but we all got free copies of the books being promoted by the featured authors. One of the more prominent publishing companies had provided the tote bag, and inside was a variety of items. All five books were included and in hardback, which I knew was a calculated expense. There were flyers and catalogs for other books and a handful of sample booklets. Other than the books, the biggest splurge was for Tom's book - a cellphone stand with the cover of his book printed on it. I made a mental note to give that to my father.

Fredrick's editor, Christi, sat at the table with me, as did Louisa, who had been assigned to help Christi that morning. There was too much tension at the table, but it was lost on Louisa.

"How do you know Tom Scott?" Louisa asked before the breakfast started.

"My father used to be his publisher, and they're still friends," I said, trying to avoid looking at the table on stage where Fredrick sat talking to Tom.

"Why aren't you his editor?" Louisa asked, picking at a muffin on her plate.

I wasn't really in the mood to answer these questions. I wanted to be alone, to think. How had I missed that Fredrick was going to be moderating this panel? How did I even forget that he would be here? Had someone deliberately kept this from me? What was he talking to Tom about? I was sure they were talking about me.

I took a deep breath and slowly exhaled. None of this was Louisa's fault, and I knew she didn't deserve to bear the brunt of my anxiety. "Tom found a new publisher before I started working," I explained.

"I think you should be his publisher," Louisa said with a sharp nod.

I smiled at her. Only in Louisa's world would it be so black and white. She knew nothing about my history with Fredrick - nobody here did. I turned to face Christi, who was glaring at me at that moment. Maybe I was wrong about nobody at the event knowing our history.

I leaned closer to Louisa, who sat between Christi and me. "I didn't realize that Fredrick's book was being promoted this week," I said to Christi.

My colleague's eyes narrowed. "We decided, since the book just came out, that we should bring him since he is kicking off his book tour here in NYC in a few days. He's doing a book signing at the booth later. You should come by," Christi said.

"OMG, Emma, you should come by. I bet it will be a zoo!" Louisa said, remaining blissfully oblivious.

I didn't say anything but pulled Fredrick's book from the tote bag and looked it over. I realized I had read this book before. In fact, it would be fair to say that I had been its first editor. Fredrick had written it the summer we met.

"This is pretty much a collection of nightmares I had as a child," Fredrick had said when he handed me the printed story ten years ago.

We lived in the same apartment for a week, and it had been weird and tense. That night, we talked and realized we were both English majors with different concentrations. I was focused on literature and criticism, but he was focused on writing. The stories had come out when he found out I was an editor for the department literary journal.

Fredrick had run into his room and come out with a stack of papers held together with a massive black binder clip. He took a deep breath, and I could hear the waiver as he exhaled before handing it to me.

"Do you want to submit them to the journal next year?" I asked as I flipped through the first few pages.

His face fell, and I knew he wasn't ready to let strangers read these. How difficult it must have been to let me read it when we barely knew each other.

"Probably not," he said before dropping on the sofa again, "but it would be great to get some feedback on them."

I stayed up all that night reading the stories. They were full of monsters, witches, and creatures. He managed to scare me, which was rare. I found areas I thought he could expand and finesse the story, thinking about what I liked from horror books when I was a kid. Our entire relationship started over those stories. It helped us grow comfortable with each other, but that was before a screenwriting class shifted his focus. He put the stories away, which was the first time I had seen them since.

Now I was listening to Fredrick talk to a room of five hundred book lovers about why he wrote his book.

"I wrote this book before I started screenwriting," he said from the podium next to the table. "With a double major in English and psychology, I was trying to see if I could bring the two worlds together. This book was my first attempt, but once I learned to write for television and movies, I found a better way to achieve what I wanted. This story was never too far from my thoughts. The first person to read it, an ex-girlfriend, provided the encouragement I needed when I needed it the most. Even though the book sat untouched for almost ten years, the support she gave me has fueled my entire career. Even now, I don't think I would be so successful if it hadn't been for her."

I was glad Tom was the first speaker after Fredrick, but he didn't make me feel much better. It was touching to hear that he didn't simply remember me as the woman who broke his heart. I had to fight back my tears, and if I hadn't been determined to hear Tom speak, I probably would have left.

Tom didn't get up to the podium. Instead, he pulled a table-top microphone closer to him, pulled his notes out of his shirt pocket, and adjusted his glasses before clearing his throat.

"This book was inspired by one of the most fascinating women I have ever met in my life," he said before looking up and meeting my eyes before giving me a small smile. "It's amazing how people change in the wake of grief. When I wrote my first novel thirty-five years ago, my editor was a young woman right out of college. She was one of the most important women in my life. Until the day she died, she was my biggest cheerleader, my biggest critic, and, after her death, one of my greatest sources of inspiration. I saw how her death changed the people she loved the most. I wondered for years what she would think of the way these people had changed. If the dead really are aware and watching over us, what would they do if they didn't like the way people changed?"

During that opening, we kept our eyes locked on each other. Tom talked more about death and grief, but I understood why he had made a point of inviting me. My mother's death had changed all four of the people she left behind. My father still lived deep within his grief. I had been dealing with it and trying to bring him out of it since I was fourteen. It was overwhelming to have both Fredrick and Tom talk about me. Hearing Tom speak about my mother right after Fredrick spoke about how important I was to his book made me realize how much I wished she had been able to help me when I graduated. While Tom spoke, I had to wipe the tears from my eyes. Once the tears started, it was impossible to keep them at bay. I quickly grabbed my bag of books, waved to the people at my table, and made my way out of the room when Tom was finished. I found a quiet bathroom (a rarity at an event like PubCon, but I knew where the best bathrooms were) and cried in a stall.

Chapter Five

I tried to hide for most of the day. I had a few appointments and took some time at lunch to walk around with Mary and grab free books. I had recognized the weird things that could happen this week, but I had no idea they would be happening to me. I wanted some time to clear my head and not think about Fredrick.

"I can't believe you didn't get me invited to the breakfast!" Mary whined as we tried to navigate the aisles of booths with heavy tote bags filled with books. "The boys would love a copy of Fredrick's book. Plus, Tom knows me too! Can I take your copy of the two books?"

I looked at my sister as if she was insane. Her sons were toddlers and had no use for a copy of Fredrick's book. "No, I would like to read them both. I think Tom's book is about Mom," I said as someone bumped into me.

"What?" Mary said with a humph. "Then why wouldn't he invite me?"

I turned away from her and started walking again, rolling my eyes once she couldn't see. "Well, it was probably because you didn't decide to come to PubCon until the last minute. Why don't you ask Louisa for her copy of Tom's book? Plus, I'm sure she can snag you a copy of Fredrick's book since she's acting as Christi's intern."

Mary stepped on the back of my sneaker as we walked, and I knew it was deliberate. "I can't believe you left me out again," she growled.

We walked back to the meeting area after lunch. We found Karen in the area scrolling through emails on her phone. I knew Mary was hoping to get a copy of something without dealing with the crowds.

"Mary, what a pleasant surprise," Karen said when she looked up.

"Can you believe that Emma went to the breakfast as Tom's guest this morning, and she didn't get me a ticket or anything?" Mary asked.

I knew my sister all too well. She wanted me to make it up to her in some way. If that meant she had to go through someone else to get my apology gift, then she would use anyone to her advantage.

"You can have my bag if you want," Karen said, handing her a bag full of the books given at breakfast.

Mary's eyes got wide as she snatched the bag out of Karen's hands. "You went too?"

Karen shook her head and looked back down at her phone. "No, there were extras. They always make extras in case more people show up than expected or if someone swipes an extra one. Christi gave me this one," Karen turned to me, and her tone softened. "Christi said Tom made you cry, Emma."

I thought about how I wanted to respond. Did she think my feelings for Fredrick had faded or was she making sure Mary didn't know my history with Fredrick? I'd never told Mary or Elizabeth about Fredrick. I never tell Elizabeth anything, and Mary was off at college herself. My father, who dismissed Fredrick as soon as he met him, never mentioned him either. As I considered my options, I felt my sister put her arm around my shoulder and pull me closer to her.

"His book is about Mom," I said, a catch in my voice.

Karen stood up and wrapped her arms around Mary and me. "So many people loved her, but you girls were her world."

I smiled and wiped the wetness away from my eyes before it could turn into tears and sat down at the table with Karen. Mary and Karen chatted about my nephews (and coerce Karen into free copies of books for my nephews), so I pulled out my phone and checked through my emails. A few manuscripts were waiting for me. I only looked up when I heard an increase of fan-girl-like squeals from my sister. Fredrick Wentworth walked into the meeting area with Christi and Louisa. Our eyes met briefly before I turned away to look at Karen. Karen's face was full of concern.

"I didn't realize they were promoting his book this week. I thought it came out already," Karen said, leaning out of Mary's earshot.

I broke eye contact with Fredrick and turned my attention to my mentor. I caught a brief flash of anger on Fredrick's face as I turned away.

"Christi felt it was a good idea since his tour starts here early next week," I said after clearing my throat.

Karen nodded, looking off behind me, probably at Fredrick. "He must be doing a signing at the booth."

I nodded. "I didn't know about any of it. He was the moderator for this morning's panel."

Karen's eyes narrowed before she looked at me again and smiled. "I hate to ask what I am about to ask then, but as your boss, I need you to staff one of the imprint booths for an hour."

"Dad's imprint?" I asked, a smile spreading across my face.

"Yes," Karen said, looking over the booth-signing schedule printed on a card that had been placed on tables around our area. "You are going to be right across from Fredrick's signing."

"OMG, Emma, will you get him to autograph a copy of the book for the boys?" Mary asked, shifting her attention back to me.

I was getting annoyed with my sister's neediness, and I knew it was because I felt overwhelmed. Plus, I didn't want to talk to Fredrick as if he was a stranger. "I am sure Louisa can get him to do that for you."

Mary, who could tell when my patience thinned, stuck her tongue out as she pulled her copy of Fredrick's book from her tote and walked over to Louisa. I couldn't help but watch. I didn't overhear anything my sister said, but Freddy's reaction was apparent, so I could make some assumptions.

"Hi!" Mary said, holding Fredrick's book out with an expectant smile on her face.

"OMG! I am so glad you're here! This is Fredrick Wentworth... you know, the screenwriter of that movie you love," Louisa said as she bounced and grabbed Mary's hand. "Freddy, I can still call you Freddy, right? Freddy, this is my sister-in-law Mary. You asked how I knew Tom at breakfast today. Well, Mary is Emma's younger sister. Tom was at Mary's wedding."

My sisters and I look alike. We all have long, chestnut brown hair, green eyes, and high cheekbones. I can only assume this made Freddy look over to me and back to Mary a few times.

Freddy took the book from Mary and quickly signed it for her. Mary returned to our table with a self-satisfied look on her face. "I'm going to walk around some more. We're getting dinner tonight, right?" She said to me.

I slowly nodded, half expecting her to gloat. "Yes."

"Good," Mary said as she grabbed her tote bags and walked out to the busy exhibit floor.

As one of the largest publishing companies in the world, we didn't have a small booth on the exhibit floor. We took over three rows of space with our smaller imprints clustered around the core autographing and meeting area. When my father sold our company, it became one of those imprints, which was why I had to sit at the booth for the entire hour of Fredrick's signing. He sat directly across from me, greeting the attendees who had lined up so he could autograph his book. It was surreal to watch women rush the booth. Some just wanted to take a picture of him, some with him, and others fought to get in line. I watched him as he smiled, talked, and signed copies of his book for each of them. Christi and Louisa kept things moving the entire time. Nobody was allowed time to chat with him, but Fredrick would look over and catch my eye every few minutes. I couldn't do anything but watch. The crowds made it impossible for anyone else to get over to the side tables where the imprints promoted their books. Each time Fredrick looked at me, I felt the tightness in my stomach that I hadn't felt in eight years.

I remembered going to parties with him and splitting up to talk to our friends. We would catch each other's eyes and smile every so often. It was our pact to help each other deal with our anxiety in large groups. I wondered if he was doing that now. I tested my theory towards the end of the hour by smiling at him when he looked over at me. He smiled back, and I saw his shoulders fall and his face relax. For the next fifteen minutes, I continued to smile at him when I saw him look over at me, and each time, he smiled back.

"What was that look?" Karen asked, returning after her lunch meeting.

I hadn't noticed she'd arrived, and I felt like a teenager caught not paying attention in class. "Testing a theory."

"What theory?" she asked, looking back and forth between Fredrick and me.

His smile faltered for a moment when he saw Karen. I sighed and focused on my boss. "Something I know about him that I'm pretty sure I'm going to have to share with Christi for his book tour."

"Emma, you made the right decision when you graduated. You do know that? If you have any regrets, it was not my intent."

I shook my head. "I don't regret my choices."

Even as I spoke the words, I was fully committed to the lie.

Chapter Six

D inner plans have changed," Mary said when she opened her hotel room door. "Tommy is here!"

I walked into the room to see my boyishly handsome brother-in-law sitting on the edge of the bed watching a baseball game. He was dressed in a polo shirt and khakis. He didn't look away from the game but lifted a hand to greet me.

"If you two want a romantic dinner in the city, I am happy to leave," I said, happy for an excuse to go home for a quiet night alone.

"Oh, no," Mary said before going back into the bathroom, where she applied her makeup. "I talked to Louisa, and she invited us to join them for dinner."

"Them?" I asked.

Mary didn't break eye contact with her mirror self. "Christi, Louisa, and Fredrick! Isn't that awesome? We are

45

going to have dinner with a famous person! My friends are going to be so jealous."

"You know tons of famous writers," I reminded her and went to sit in the armchair across the room.

Mary poked her head out of the bathroom door. "Writers aren't famous, EMMA!"

"Fredrick is a writer."

"But in Hollywood."

I rolled my eyes and took a deep breath. Twenty-four hours ago, Fredrick Wentworth had been a memory. Now my sister was latching onto him like he was the second coming. It was like I was trying to manifest the end. I knew this would be over once PubCon ended, and I focused on getting through the next couple of days.

This wasn't the worst dinner of my life, but it was up there on the list. The worst dinner of my life was technically the first after my mother died. The second worst was the big family dinner the night of graduation, days after Fredrick had proposed, when I realized I was going to say no. This dinner wasn't nearly as bad as those two. I'm sure it was because I drank more wine than I should have. Wine typically makes me more aggressive and talkative. I find myself oversharing. It was challenging to get a word between Mary, Louisa, and Christi, even if I had something to say.

"I wish I could go on a book tour," Mary said.

"Oh, we normally don't go with authors," Christi said, waving her hand to dismiss Mary. "I mean, we usually advise their publicists about what to do, and we coordinate from our offices. Fredrick is a rare case because he's a celebrity."

Mary met my eye and raised her eyebrow as if this had proven her earlier point.

"Did you know that Emma is the queen of book tours?" Christi continued without noticing the look my sister gave me. "She often plans them, even if she doesn't go on them. If someone needs to go with a famous author, she typically does. I think I went with you one time, Emma. I remember being really bored and exhausted."

I thought about the time we had gone to Boston with a celebrity author who had been anxious about what to expect. After that first stop, she sent us back to New York. It was rarely exciting since most bookstores and publicists knew what they were doing.

"Why?" Louisa asked. She had always wanted to go to a book event with me, and now she was going to find out why I never invited her.

Christi smirked. "You basically spend all your time preparing for the reading and signing. You're exhausted from travel to the point where you just want to go to bed when the signing is over. The next day you repeat it all over again in a new town or city and bookstore. Fredrick, be ready," Christi said.

"Is this true, Emma?" Louisa asked me.

"Absolutely," I said. "Sometimes the editor goes to any signing in New York City since we are here already. Authors have publicists who travel with them."

"If you and the author have a good relationship, you can try to make it somewhat enjoyable," Christi said before leaning close to the table. "One author, who I won't name, likes to play fashion police with the people who come in for the signings. Most authors spend their time worrying if people will show up to the reading."

"Don't people come to all the readings?" Mary asked, her eyes wide.

I chuckled as Christi shook her head. "Not necessarily. There are so many uncontrollable factors. PubCon is nice because you can start promoting some books to librarians, pushing new authors. The newer the author, the more difficult it is to get people to show up. Not everyone gets promoted here, and smaller publishers don't always have the resources to promote like we do."

"Are you nervous, Freddy?" Louisa asked, turning to look at him.

I watched Fredrick wince ever so slightly. I knew he didn't like being called Freddy. His mother and father had only called him Fredrick. I was the only one who ever called him Freddy, and that was something intimate. He often corrected people who made the mistake, but he would be spending the next month with Louisa. He was probably trying to find the right time to ask her to cease calling him Freddy. I caught his eye and gave him a reassuring smile. This time he did not smile back.

"A bit, obviously. I think at least two people will show up to each of the signings," Fredrick said.

"I hope more than two," Christi said with a bark of a laugh. "If today is any indication of what to expect,

I think your signings will be popular. We've contact-
ed all the bookstores about security help, ticketing for
lines, and general midnight-release-of-Harry-Potter management. This is why you and I are running this tour,
Louisa."

"You are asking them to treat him like Harry Potter?"
Mary said, her eyebrows scrunching together.

"It's more of a level of consideration," I said, touching
my sister's hand.

Mary looked at me and nodded.

"Book stores everywhere did midnight releases and understand what it means when we want that type of crowd
management," Christi said.

"To change the subject," Tommy said as he stifled a yawn.
"Fredrick, since you have a few days to yourself here in
New York City, what do you plan on doing?"

I was more than happy to shift to a new topic. My brother-in-law had no interest in publishing, and I was sure he
was bored. I was anxious that Fredrick might bring up
something about our shared past, something nobody had
mentioned yet. Listening to Christi talk about how much I
was relied on to help with book tours only made me aware
of how little time I spent doing the part of publishing I
loved, editing the books. I was eight years into a career and
still helping plan book tours when our marketing department and publicity teams should be handling all of that.
No wonder I hadn't progressed as much as I expected.

"I was thinking of seeing the sights over the weekend,"
Fredrick said, not missing a beat. I was sure he was tired
of the book tour conversation too. "The first signing is on

Monday afternoon, and my publicist, Patrick, isn't getting here until Sunday."

"Don't you think people will recognize you?" Tommy asked.

Fredrick shrugged. "Usually, people have no idea who I am until someone tells them or if I'm with another celebrity. It's weird but refreshing to be able to walk around and be a normal person."

I had a momentary thought about what his life would be like if I had gone to California with him and we had gotten married. Would he be famous at all? I didn't think I would enjoy that life.

"We're staying in the city for a few days," Mary said, sitting up in her chair, aware of her opportunity. "We would love to take you around. Emma, you should join us too!"

I was sure my panic showed on my face. "I have to be back at PubCon tomorrow," I said, not wanting to spend any more time with Fredrick than necessary.

"What about Sunday?" Mary whined.

I shook my head as my mind populated all the possible excuses I could use. "With Dad and Elizabeth's move, PubCon, and getting ready for Cape Cod next month, I haven't had a chance to do things around my own apartment. I need to get back to normal."

"You're a party pooper," Mary pouted.

Chapter Seven

I didn't get to PubCon until after lunch on Saturday. Since I had already been there two days and didn't have any appointments, I wasn't in a rush to get there. Plus, this was the day the general public was allowed to attend. If the first two days had been chaotic, Saturday was a clusterfuck. I arrived at the booth to find people in a state of panic. There were cops, firefighters, and paramedics scattered around our booth. I hoped to avoid the public who might act entitled to free books.

"Emma, you missed it!" Karen said when she saw me. She was out of breath, and her hand rested over her heart.

"What happened?" I asked, looking around as I made sense of the panic around us.

Karen pointed to a pile of Fredrick's books scattered on the floor. The dark blue animated cover had pops of silver that glistened in the right lights. "Christi got into an argument with an attendee."

I felt my anxiety rise. This was precisely why I had arrived late. "What? Why? Has someone been arrested?"

"It was over copies of Fredrick's book," Karen said and stepped out of the path of walkers who were making their way down the aisle again. "We ran out of copies, and some of the general public attendees got really angry. This is just the worst thing that's ever happened!"

"So, Christi was arrested?"

Karen shook her head and leaned closer to me. "No, a couple of attendees got really aggressive and ganged up on her. They broke her arm and a leg. We will have a meeting in an hour to discuss Fredrick's tour. She can't manage the tour now."

I sighed and hoped this meant that Fredrick could travel on his tour with just his publicist like other authors do. "Do you need me at the booth while the meeting is going on?"

Karen pointed to the woman talking to people and waving her arms as the man next to her handed out boxes. I looked around and saw people beginning to pull books off the displays and start offering them to people. I wasn't accustomed to the sense of urgency for this conference.

"No, we're packing up early because of this," Karen said with a sigh. "We may have a lawsuit against the convention organizers for lack of security. We'll deal with that later. I need you at the meeting."

"What? Why?"

She leaned closer to me and whispered. "You know Fredrick, and you know book tours for popular authors."

I bit back all the things I wanted to say. I was sure Karen would keep me away from whatever happened with his tour.

The impromptu meeting was a mess. Some executives wanted to talk about legal action against the conference organizers. Others wanted to talk about Christi's responsibilities, primarily Fredrick's book tour. As they all talked over each other, I sat in the background, barely paying attention until I heard my name.

"Emma should do it," said some executive I didn't know.

"Excuse me?" I asked, shocked to hear my name.

"You should take Christi's place on tour," he said as I tried to recall his name without success. "You've done tours in the past. Fredrick is important, and we want to make sure we have a presence on his tour."

"I have my own authors to handle," I added barely after he had finished speaking. I could feel the panic rising as my body got warmer.

"I am sure Karen can help pick up those duties," one of the other executives said, and the rest nodded in agreement.

"Um," I said and turned to Karen for help, who sat there with her eyes closed.

"I can help finish those projects that require help," Karen said after taking a deep breath. "But I know Emma can do the work while on tour."

I was stunned into silence. She knew exactly who Fredrick was to me and should be fighting to keep me home.

"We've spoken with Fredrick's publicist, Patrick," Christi's boss said. "He was already going on the tour. We're going to send Louisa with you since she helped Christi through the conference."

I realized I had been set up. The decision had been made before the meeting had started, maybe even before I had arrived that morning.

"Is he really that important that we need an editor and an intern to help his publicist?" someone asked.

I looked around the room but didn't see the lone voice of reason.

"Yes!" was the response, and all conversation ended.

My mind spun as I fought to keep my panic and anxiety from overwhelming me. I didn't know how I would spend a month with Fredrick Wentworth, making sure everything was to his satisfaction.

"I am so sorry," Karen said when we left the convention floor.

"I need to get home and pack," I said, not ready to have this conversation with her. "I guess I should go see Christi tomorrow and make sure I'm ready for Monday," I said, trying to take control of the situation.

I plowed through the crowd, weaving my way through the clusters of people still collecting free books or talking to vendors. Karen rushed to keep up with me, but I didn't wait for her.

"Emma, do you want to talk about this?" she asked, making sure she was heard above the crowd. "I recognize that yesterday was difficult, seeing Fredrick after all this time. I'm worried about you spending a month with him."

I didn't say anything. I was too busy planning things in my mind.

"Emma, please talk to me," Karen said when I didn't respond.

"For all your concern, you didn't stop them from forcing me to spend a month traveling with him," I said, turning my head for a moment. "Also, I had dinner with him last night."

"Alone?" She asked.

I shook my head. "No, Christi, Louisa, Mary, and Tommy were all there. I'm pretty sure he hates me. Has anyone talked to him yet? Is he ok with me taking over?"

"Yes, his publicist said Fredrick agreed."

I gave a curt nod. "Will you check in on Dad and Elizabeth?"

"Of course I will. Are you sure you don't want to talk about this?"

I stopped and turned to Karen as we exited the exhibit floor and was able to get away from the crowd. "Did he know before me?" I asked.

"Know what?" Karen asked as she nodded her head a little.

"That I would replace Christi? I'm getting the impression the decision had been made before that meeting started."

Karen walked away from me and started walking toward the doors outside. "Yes, he knew before you did."

Chapter Eight

I went directly to the hospital and met with Christi to go over the details of the tour. She looked relaxed, and I assumed it was the drugs. Her right leg was in a cast and elevated with a sling. Her right arm was in another cast. If she was in pain, I couldn't tell. Her mind was sharp, and she was able to tell me everything I needed to know about the tour. We were undisturbed while we talked.

"You start here with morning shows, a party at the New York Public Library, and one signing at Barnes and Noble," she told me from her hospital bed.

"Nothing else in New York?"

She shook her head. "Not until the end of the tour. From here, you go to Boston for a few days. That is mostly readings and signings and an interview with the Boston Globe."

"Brookline Booksmith is included, I presume," I said with a smile, thinking of the independent bookstore just outside of Boston.

"They rented the theater across the street for him," Christi said as she adjusted her pillow a little. "The tickets sold out fast. The only other venue to sell tickets was Los Angeles, but that's because of local notoriety. After Boston, you go down to DC. Again there will be signings and newspapers."

"Ok."

"After DC, you go to Atlanta. The same will go on there, and this is the farthest south you will travel."

"Not Miami?" I asked, without looking up from my planner where I was taking notes.

Christi rolled her eyes. "No, Books and Books wouldn't agree to what we asked."

"What did you ask of them?"

"We wanted the reading in the courtyard," she said and shrugged.

I jerked my head up. "Christi, Miami in June is hot as all hell. What were you thinking?"

"It's the only space they have that could accommodate the crowd. The bookstore is already crowded, and they refused to find another space."

"Did they think the crowd would be smaller?" I asked as I drew my eyebrows together.

My colleague shook her head. "No, they just wanted it in the store with the space they have."

"Ok, so no Miami," I said, looking back at my planner again.

"From Atlanta, you go to LA, and you'll be there the longest. I mean, other than New York City."

I had never been to Los Angeles, which was the city I was most nervous about visiting. If I had married Fredrick eight years ago, that's where we would live. I was sure all his friends knew about me and had already judged me.

"We spend three days in each city, without the travel time. How much time in LA?" I asked, trying to figure out if I could find other things to fill my time.

"A full week," Christi said as she counted the days on her fingers and took a deep breath. "He's going to hit bookstores and parties every night. They're doing a huge launch party with some of the big bookstores. It will be for celebrities only. His friends want to throw a party for him. All the local news shows are interviewing him. A library asked him to run a writing workshop for teens. They are connecting it to some National Novel Writing Month event. I thought that was in November, but they said July."

I nodded. "They do smaller writing events in April and July. They call it Camp NaNoWriMo."

"How do you know?"

"I pay attention to when people are writing. We've found amazing books through participants," I said with a sheepish smile.

Christi gave me a look that I thought was annoyance. I wanted to assume that she was simply irritated that I would be on the tour she had expected to lead, but there had been tension between us before her accident. I wanted to remind her that I was just as unhappy about this as she

SARA MARKS

was, but I kept my mouth shut. It would only make this tension worse.

"Right. So, he agreed to run the workshop. Five days there and travel time. From there, you're on to Chicago because he went to college there. Then you return to New York City, and I should be well enough to take over so you can go on your vacation."

I instinctually grimaced. I had been so busy mentally preparing myself for Los Angeles that I hadn't prepared myself for Chicago, the city where we had been together. I could feel, in my stomach, the flutters of all my repressed emotions. There was no way I could stop them from coming to the surface, but I had to find a way to cope.

"What am I specifically responsible for?" I asked, hoping she would help me without knowing it.

"The publicist, his name is Patrick, is taking care of almost everything. Apparently, he works with big-name authors and actors. He knows his stuff. You're a glorified and expensive babysitter. All you have to be at are the bookstore signings. Your job is dealing with the books, so treat each city like you treat New York City signings."

"What's Louisa going to do? I don't really need her help," I said, aware that even Christi thought I was the book tour guru.

Christi fiddled with the TV remote, and I wondered if something was being kept from me. "Essentially, you are there to make sure the bookstores are happy. Louisa was helping me plan the tour, so she's spoken with managers to plan these events. She's going to make sure those people feel comfortable."

60

I narrowed my eyes. None of this made sense. Yes, Fredrick was a celebrity, but this level of support was unprecedented. "Why isn't Louisa going instead of me?"

Christi didn't look me in the eyes as she shrugged. Whatever the real reason, I wasn't going to get it from her.

Even though we would be in town for another three days, the tour officially kicked off Monday morning. I left Christi to start packing, stopping for supplies I knew I would need for the various events. Once I got home, I opened my closet, dropped to the floor, and spent an hour crying. Returning to New York after graduation had been difficult. I had compartmentalized my emotions over leaving Fredrick but focused on my father's needs and work. After the past few days, it was getting difficult to keep all these emotions locked away. I had to remember to keep them locked away until I was alone. I would probably have plenty of moments like this for the next month.

"You are the Queen of book tours," I said to my reflection in the bathroom mirror as I cleaned up. "Get into the game. He isn't your Freddy anymore. He's Fredrick Wentworth, who has never been on a book tour and has no idea what he has agreed to do. You will make him think it's effortless and keep him calm. Now, get your head out of your ass, pack what you need, and get ready to meet his team tomorrow morning. Who cares if his publicist knows what happened eight years ago. You are both professionals."

I couldn't help but notice that even my pep-talk had a mocking undertone. It was enough to help me focus, and I pulled out clothes, toiletries, and supplies. My shoes (many swiped from Elizabeth's extensive collection) filled one bag alone. I even pulled out the fancy dress I decided to wear to the New York Public Library's $1,000 a plate fundraiser party. I made a mental note to let Patrick know this was black-tie.

I was exhausted and starving by the time I finished preparations. I was rooting through my collection of take-out menus when the outside buzzer went off.

"Hello?"

"Emma! Come for a walk with us!" Louisa said through the intercom.

I buzzed them up, forgetting that Fredrick was with them.

"We brought Patrick along so you could meet him!" Louisa said to me when all five were stuffed inside the front room.

Mary and Tommy stood off to the side, and Fredrick glared at me. Standing next to him was a rail-thin brunette man about the same height as Fredrick. He wore thick rectangular glasses and had a square jaw.

"So, you are the infamous Emma Shaw," Patrick said, extending his hand to shake mine.

"Infamous?" I asked and raised an eyebrow.

I turned to Fredrick, but he gave nothing away. His eyes were busy looking around my apartment. My wall of bookcases was filled with books and knick-knacks. There were pictures of Mary and Tommy on their wedding day, my nephews, my parent's wedding, Karen and me when I graduated high school, and my favorite pictures of my mother. Actually, there were more pictures of my mother than anyone else. Mary loved my picture collection because there was only one of Elizabeth (actually one of three of us when we were little) and many of Mary and her family. She claimed it as a win.

"Christi called you the Queen of Book Tours," Patrick said.

"Right," I said and let out a sigh. I had been nervous about why I was so infamous.

"I'm here to just help in any way I can," Patrick said with a wink.

That wasn't how Christi made it out, but we didn't need to deal with that tonight.

"As long as you have tuxes!" I said, thinking I was making a joke.

"Why?" Patrick said, looking confused.

"Tuesday night," I said, looking rapidly between Fredrick and Patrick. "New York Public Library? The black-tie benefit? Fredrick is the guest of honor? Do you know about this?"

I could feel my face getting hot. I suddenly wanted to get out of this room. Had none of this been communicated to Patrick? Was this going to be a mess before we even got started?

"I was unaware it was black tie," Patrick said, putting his finger to his lips.

"I have a tux with me," Fredrick said, his voice flat.

"I can take care of it, Patrick!" Louisa quickly said. "Tomorrow, after the morning show, we'll go to a tailor I know. He can get something ready for you by Tuesday afternoon."

"Perfect!" Patrick said, a smile spreading over his face. "Right now, I've been on a flight all day, eaten my fill of tapas, and I need ice cream."

I was glad he had suggested going out because I suddenly wanted everyone out of my home and to breathe fresh air. "I haven't had dinner yet, and there are a few things to do tonight, but I can walk to Columbus Circle with you. There's a Pink Berry there."

Mary clapped her hands and squealed in delight. I grabbed my purse and pushed everyone out the door.

Even though Mary walked beside me during the mile walk from my apartment to Columbus Circle, I didn't really pay attention to whatever it was she prattled on about. With everything that had gone on over the last few days, my patience was thin, and I needed to be alone to recharge. Patrick and Tommy walked at the front of the group discussing whatever they had to talk about. Louisa and Fredrick walked in the center of the group. I was trying not to listen, but Louisa was flirting as if her life depended on it. Fredrick allowed her to go on and on about how amazing New York was, how the tour would be amazing even without Christi, how funny he was, how terrible his last breakup must have been, and how she was going to take care of him over the next month.

"I'm exhausted from all this walking," Mary said when we arrived at Columbus Circle.

The walk had been less than a mile.

"Why don't you go sit, and I'll get you some yogurt," Tommy said and wrapped his arms around her.

"Oh, Emma, let's go sit at the fountain!" Mary said, squirming away from him and grabbing my hand.

I let my sister pull me onto the crosswalk. Nobody followed us, but I still let my sister lead me to the edge of the flowing fountain.

"My feet are killing me after PubCon," Mary said as she sat down on the ledge.

"Understandable," I said, refusing to sit. "I need to get something for dinner, Mary. I can't stay."

Mary pulled off her shoes and stretched her feet. "Just wait here with me until the others come back, and then you can go grab something for dinner. Please, Emma."

I would never hear the end of it if I left Mary alone. So, I gave up on plans for dinner and sat down while Mary continued to talk to me. I checked my phone as emails and text messages kept coming in about book tour details. After about twenty minutes, the group came back with yogurt and more. Louisa walked arm and arm with Fredrick, and he laughed at something she said. I felt a punch to my gut and bit back my desire to say something snippy. I spent a month with Fredrick and the rest of my life with Louisa.

Tommy made his way over to Mary and handed her a cup of yogurt. After taking a take-out container from Fredrick, Patrick sat down next to me and gave it to me.

"We thought you could use something of substance since we kidnapped you away from dinner," Patrick said with a smile.

"Thank you," I said, surprised by the kindness.

"We had a small debate," Patrick said and made sure to look into my eyes. "Louisa and Tommy thought Starbucks and yogurt would be fine. I saw a hole-in-the-wall Chinese place since those places can be good. But Fredrick saw a Mediterranean place and thought falafel would be the best pick. Plus, they had an 'A' in the window, and the Chinese place didn't have any letter."

"I really appreciate this," I said with a smile.

I opened the container to find falafel, hummus, pita, and a salad. I looked up and smiled at Fredrick. He only nodded in response and turned his attention back to Louisa. I looked at Patrick, who smirked. I had no doubt that he knew exactly who I was to Fredrick.

Chapter Nine

I remember the first time Fredrick kissed me. After a month of being roommates, our relationship had evolved into a casual friendship. We shared the things we had in common and told each other the important details of our lives. I knew he was an only child with parents who spoiled him and taught him to be independent. He knew about my family and the impact my mother's death had on our dynamic. When we realized how much we both loved the original Star Wars trilogy, we decided to watch all three movies in one night. We settled on the couch with pizza, beer, and snacks on Saturday afternoon. Within the first thirty minutes, it became a drinking game. By the end of the Empire Strikes Back, we were keeping each other upright. I was intoxicated enough for my self-conscious restraint to slip away, and I was acting on impulse. After weeks of fantasizing about what it would be like to kiss Fredrick, I decided it was time to find out. I swung myself across him so that I straddled him and pressed my lips to his.

It was awkward for the first few seconds, but we found a rhythm when I felt his hands grasp my hips. When I moved my hands under his t-shirt, he let me lift it off. I felt his hands roam over my back, but he didn't try to unhook my bra. When he stood up, I wrapped my legs around his hips and giggled while still kissing him. He stumbled a few times, but he didn't let go until he was standing at the foot of my bed. I unhooked my legs and fell back. I pushed myself back toward my pillow, and he crawled onto the bed until he was over me again. Between kisses, I let him take off my jeans. When I tried to take off his pants, he stopped and pulled away.

"What? I want this. I want you," I said, still breathing heavily.

Fredrick shook his head. "No, not like this."

I reached for him, ready to pull him back to me, "Yes, like this. This is the way I want it."

"You are drunk," he said and moved away from me before I could get him in my grasp.

"So?"

"I don't want our first time together to be while we're drunk," he said as he sat on the edge of the bed.

"It's going to be a mess anyway. The first time together is never graceful," I said, positioning myself behind him and kissing his neck.

He let me do this for a moment before forcing himself to his feet. "If you regret it, then it becomes rape. You're not in the right frame of mind to make the right decision. If you still want this when we're sober, then there is no way I will say no. Right now, like this, I can't do it. I am not that kind of guy."

My face got hot, and I pouted. "For fuck's sake, you keep giving me reasons to like you. Why can't you just be that guy right now when I have no inhibitions!"

He sat down in the chair at my desk, leaning his elbows on his knees and putting his face in his hands. "Because I have been fantasizing about you since we met. I don't want a one-night stand when I have to live here for the rest of the year. I want you so much."

I felt my anger dissipate. "Sex fantasies?" I asked and raised an eyebrow.

"Well, among others," he said, giving me a sheepish grin.

"Others?" I asked, and a smile spread across my face.

He moved back to the bed and sat next to me, taking my hand in his. "I want everything. I have fantasies about what our first fight would be about. I have fantasies about cuddling in bed, reading books, and playing footsies."

I knew kissing him had been the right decision. We wanted the same thing, and it was surprisingly arousing to learn about his cute relationship fantasies. "Really?" I asked as I ran my free hand through his hair. "You do know this all just turns me on even more."

He removed my hand and put it in my lap. "Please, Emma," he said, practically whispering. "I want you. I want to kiss you and touch you and love you. You will wake up in the morning, probably hungover, and I will still want you. You don't need to be drunk to feel confident enough to make a move. If you wake up and still want me, then you will know where I am and that I will still want you too."

With that, he got up, left, and went to his own room.

I heard him walking to the bathroom once I was in bed. I waited until I heard the bathroom door open.

"Freddy," I called into the hallway.

"What's up?" he said, walking to my doorway.

"Sleep in here, with me."

"Emma."

"I promise nothing until morning. I just..." I said and swallowed so I could speak clearly. "I want to know what it's like to sleep next to you and to wake up in your arms. That's been my fantasy."

He didn't say anything as he got into the bed with me. I did just as I promised. I could feel the warmth of his breath on the back of my neck and his hand draped over my waist. I fell asleep with him spooning me.

The next morning I woke up buried in his body after rolling over in the night. His arms were around me, our legs entwined, and my face in his neck. I could hear him gently snoring. I lay there in his arms, exploring what I could of his body. He smelled like musk and oranges. I counted freckles on his shoulder and looked at scars to determine what they could have been from. I even looked for moles before he began to stir.

"Good morning," I whispered when he opened his eyes.

A sleepy smile spread across his face. "Good morning."

"Nothing has changed. I want what I want."

He let me pull off his clothes this time, and we made love for the first time.

It was a mess, but it was also everything I had wanted it to be.

Chapter Ten

Patrick dealt with the early morning shows without me. He assured me that he and Fredrick did these all the time to promote movies. We agreed to meet at the Columbus Circle Barnes & Noble for the first book signing later that afternoon to set up together. Not getting up before the sun didn't stop me from watching the morning shows to watch what happened. The interviews went off without a hitch for most of the shows. Since we were at the start of the book tour, we focused on the popular national morning shows. The anchors asked about the book and not Fredrick's personal life. Christi's email showed that she made a point of asking them to do this. Only one host asked about the incident of PubCon and what it was like there. Fredrick brushed it off, explaining he hadn't been there, and I mentally thanked him for trying to minimize it. The only hiccup occurred on one of the later morning shows. Their newest anchor apparently didn't care about Christi's instructions.

The anchor looked down at his note cards and smirked before looking directly into Fredrick's eyes. "You recently had a pretty bad breakup with Abby."

My stomach clenched even though I was sitting on my sofa. I wasn't sure if it was anxiety at the man's unwillingness to stay on script or because I didn't want to hear about Fredrick's other relationships.

"These things happen," Fredrick said with a shrug, the smile never wavering.

The host raised an eyebrow. "It surprised a lot of people considering that she has a child, and you seemed to really be in a good place together."

Fredrick looked down and shut his eyes for a beat. "Things change in relationships. People change, and it requires that you change the relationship."

I was sure Fredrick had been anticipating someone asking him about this. I wondered what he would have said to deflect morning show hosts if he had been this famous when we had broken up.

This man wasn't going to give up. He leaned forward and pointed a finger at Fredrick. "Abby has commented that you refused to leave Los Angeles when she wanted to make New York City her permanent home."

"That was one of many reasons," Fredrick said, his sheepish grin spreading across his face.

I heard my phone ping from its spot on my coffee table.

Patrick: Don't worry, I'm going to give the producers a piece of my mind.

I didn't respond. I didn't know if he reassured me because I'm Fredrick's publisher or his ex. I was confident that Patrick knew our past, but I wasn't sure Patrick wanted to protect me.

The anchor sat back up and laughed, the tension broken while I had been reading the text. "Well, I know there are thousands of women out there who would love to take her place. What should all the women of the world know is your number one barrier to a lasting relationship?"

Fredrick sat there for a moment, thinking. "That's a great question. I have to say the number one barrier in a lasting relationship with me is a weakness of character. If a woman can easily be persuaded by her friends and family to do something she doesn't really want, then she and I won't make a good pair."

I sat there looking at the television, and I realized I was never going to be able to fix the mistake I had made. This next month was going to be torture.

I was already at Barnes & Noble with Louisa when Fredrick and Patrick arrived. I dealt with the bookstore manager and staff to make sure the space had everything ready. I assigned Louisa to make sure Fredrick was comfortable and had what he needed. I didn't want to sit with Fredrick. After what he had said that morning, I was sure I was the last person he wanted to spend time with.

Louisa beamed as we split our tasks. "I'm happy to help you however I can, Emma. I want to learn as much as you can teach me about book tours. Think of me as the future Princess of book tours," she said at rapid speed.

This was an opportunity to teach Louisa and minimize my interaction with Fredrick. Yet, my patience was thin. Too much had happened in the past week, and I hadn't had time to stop and process it all. I planned to turn over most of the work to Louisa as the tour progressed. A part of me was so angry at Karen and the other executives that I was ready to technically comply with the assignment but to put in no effort. That was unlikely to happen because I wouldn't throw Louisa into this without help. There was still a voice in my head challenging me to do it. As Louisa went on about being the Princess of book tours, I realized I could frame this as a learning experience.

"What if you do more of the work than I do?" I asked as we brought boxes of books out to the table where Fredrick would sign autographs. "You have an idea of what Christi was going to do. I'll work with you and be your backup."

"Really!?" Louisa said, trying to bounce while holding the heavy box of books.

Her excitement was contagious. For a moment, I felt hopeful that her energy and flexibility would make everyone much happier. I decided right then if this worked out, I would make sure she had a permanent job. I just had to keep her thinking that this was only about her learning and getting experience.

I walked around the bookstore with my iPad and checklist, ensuring we had plenty of copies of books, plenty of space for a large crowd, plenty of sharpies, prizes to give away, and plenty of drinks. Louisa walked with me and her own iPad checklist. I explained all the aspects of the set-up as we worked. I didn't stop to think as I walked over to the cafe and ordered coffees and teas for the four of us. I knew Louisa drank hers with lots of milk and sugar. Patrick had made a joke the night before, as he showed me pictures of his husband Victor, that he liked his men like he liked his coffee: black and hot. I ordered Fredrick's on instinct: venti earl grey tea with raw sugar. Louisa and I brought the drinks back to the group and handed them out. Fredrick looked surprised when he took the cup from me. Our fingers touched quickly as he grabbed the cup, and I felt the jolt of electricity between us. I turned on my heel and walked back out to the main floor, fighting back the tears from emotions I thought had died years ago.

"She always seems to know what people like to drink," Louisa said as I left.

After that, I stayed away from the break room.

Once the reading began, I sat in the back and let the bookstore manager do the introductions. The room was filled with middle school and tween boys with their parents or nannies. All but one copy of the book had already been sold. While Fredrick did his reading, I rapidly called the office, requesting that another box be sent over quickly. By the time the signing started, two more boxes had been delivered, and I had stopped feeling anxious. We sold more books as people kept trickling in during the signing. As the line progressed, I sat about ten feet away from Fredrick.

"Well, I think Queen of Book Tours is an appropriate title for you," Patrick said, sitting down next to me with another coffee in his hand.

SARA MARKS

I blushed. "Thank you. You seemed to have had a pretty good morning."

"Aside from that one relationship comment, I think it was great. I did speak to the producer about that one."

I shrugged. "He handled it well."

Patrick took a long sip of his coffee before answering. "He's gotten used to relationship questions."

Every ten minutes, Fredrick would look over at where Patrick and I were sitting. I didn't know which one of us he was looking at the first few times. I smiled at him anyway. When he smiled back and seemed to relax, I knew the one job I would have, no matter what else I tried to pass on to Louisa.

Patrick turned to me with a raised eyebrow. "Oh, you're good. You may be the Empress of Book Tours."

"What?" I asked, blinking rapidly and turning to him.

He lifted his chin in Fredrick's direction. "Dealing with social anxiety issues? This many people really make him anxious. I hate having to anchor to him, but you do it naturally."

I turned back to watch Fredrick, not wanting to make eye contact with Patrick. "I'm not doing anything."

He let out a low chuckle. "Look, Emma, I know. You clearly haven't told people, but he has. I know all of it. He's not just a client. He's my best friend."

He was right. I hadn't told anyone at home about the most important relationship of my life. There had been no point. This confirmed that I needed to assume everyone in Los Angeles would know who I was to Fredrick.

"I appreciate your loyalty to him," I whispered, not sure what else to say.

Patrick put his hand on my arm and lowered his voice. "When I came out, he was the one who stood by me. He introduced me to Victor. I love him like a brother. I knew he was in love with you before you knew he was in love with you. I knew he was going to propose before you did."

I took a deep breath and turned back to Patrick. "He never talked about his friends in LA."

"Maybe you just didn't hear him. I get the impression you compartmentalize things."

I didn't know what to say in response to this. I thought about it quickly, speeding through the times we had talked about our lives beyond the borders of Chicago. I had kept plenty of details from him as if I always knew things would end once we graduated. Had he never told me about his friends, or had I ignored what he had said, assuming I would never meet them?

"Don't worry, I am here to keep the peace," Patrick said when I didn't respond. "Feel free to use your intimate knowledge of him to make this tour easier. I understand you're not here by choice. So far, you have been more amazing than I ever dreamed. You have been professional, attentive, and focused."

I shifted in my seat. "Why are you telling me this?"

Patrick took a deep breath. "I don't want to play games, and it's clear someone around you is. It's been eight years, and a lot has changed for both of you. I appreciate the effort you're making and how gracefully you've handled this so far. He's incapable of acknowledging all of that right now, but you need to hear it."

I looked down at my hands, trying to remember the last time anyone I worked with had said these things to me. "Thank you," I whispered.

Chapter Eleven

I felt more confident as I prepared for the New York Public Library benefit dinner the next day. Louisa and I went there after the second reading and signing. The items we donated for the auction had all arrived. We checked little details before going to the salon for a quick style, mani, and pedi. I got back to the apartment, got dressed, and took a cab to the library. I was pleased with my dress. The full A-line skirt was embroidered with black flowers. I wore my mother's pearl necklace and pearl clips in my hair that had been pulled back in a bun. My black open-toe shoes showed off my bright red toenails. I looked good but understated, so I would blend easily. When I walked into the large library doors, I found Fredrick sitting in his tux on a bench at the foot of the stairs that led up to the room where the benefit was taking place.

"Wow!" I heard from my left and turned to see Patrick walking toward us, his phone in his hand.

"Thanks," I said as I walked up to them, my face turning pink.

"I am going to get Louisa. She just sent me a text saying she's almost here. Wait here with Fredrick," Patrick said before walking away again.

I sighed and turned to Fredrick, whose bow tie was crooked. He started to get to his feet.

"Sit, I have to fix your tie," I said and stood in front of him.

"When did you learn to tie a bow tie?" Fredrick asked, his eyebrows knitting together.

"Oh, Freddy," I whispered and let out a small sigh. "I've always known. This is my world."

He said nothing and looked straight ahead (and later, I realized right into my cleavage) while I fiddled, making sure his tie was perfect. When I was done, I took a deep breath and inhaled the musky orange scent that I've always associated with him.

"Oh, Emma, you look so pretty!" I heard Louisa say as she walked up to us.

I turned to find her in a slinky red dress and garish red heels. Again, her shoe choice made me question her taste.

"You do as well," I lied.

To be fair, Louisa was a whole foot shorter than Fredrick and needed the three-inch heels to gain some height. She was also comfortable in high heels from years of wearing them. I was sure she would feel out of place in flats. I stepped back and watched as Louisa took Fredrick's arm. As the two walked up the stairs, I turned to Patrick, who offered me his arm.

"My Empress," he said.

I had to chuckle as I took his arm and let him lead me to the party.

I wish the party had been problem-free. I don't think most of the people there knew about the hiccup because Patrick and I shut it down as quickly as possible. While Louisa never left Fredrick's side, Patrick and I slid into the background and enjoyed ourselves quietly. We made jokes about some of the fashion choices, suggested the other try a specific food option, swiped glasses of champagne from passing waiters, and danced when the band played a good song.

"Fuck me," I heard him say under his breath at one point.

I raised my eyebrow, positive he wasn't suggesting that to me. I turned, expecting to see some handsome man walking in, but instead, there was a pixie-like, blonde woman walking right toward Fredrick.

"I don't think she's your type," I said.

"No, that's Abby," Patrick said, taking my hand and walking toward the other woman. "What's she doing here? Do you think she knows Fredrick's here?"

I was surprised I hadn't recognized her. She had changed her hairstyle and color since I had last paid attention. She was a famous actress, but I had stopped following her when she started dating Fredrick.

"If she doesn't, then she's a moron," I said, letting Patrick drag me towards her. "The library promoted the benefit, and his face was everywhere."

"She's trying to mess with his head. Help me keep her away."

I wondered why Patrick was taking me with him. Maybe it was for moral support or to have someone block her way into the party? I had a brief thought that he wanted me to see my competition for Fredrick's least favorite ex-girlfriend.

"Abby, let's talk," Patrick said as he spun her around and walked her out the door.

"What the hell? Patrick, you have no right to manhandle me," Abby said, trying to fight her way back into the room.

I stood behind Patrick but didn't do anything to help him. I had to agree with Abby.

"Oh, please, I know why you're here," Patrick said and let her go. "Let's not pretend. You've done enough to hurt him."

"He forced my hand. I told him right away that Los Angeles wasn't the life I wanted. He stayed with me anyway."

"You could've been mature about it," Patrick said, his face getting red. "You could've walked away when you knew he would never leave LA. You used your kid to keep him around. Why are you even here? You married someone else."

I took a small step back. It felt like these were the things Patrick would have said to me if we had met outside of this tour. That bit of movement caught Abby's attention, and she turned to look at me.

"I just want to talk to him. Who's this?" Abby said, pointing at me.

"Emma, the editor running his book tour," Patrick said with a shrug.

"Emma? This is Emma? The infamous Emma? You want to talk about playing games with Fredrick, and she stands here helping you keep me away."

I suddenly wanted to punch her in the face. Now I knew why Patrick dragged me over. He tried to intimidate her and make sure she knew what happened to the women who broke Fredrick's heart.

"She's doing her job, and that's making sure this all runs smoothly," Patrick said in a whisper. "She's not the one causing a scene. You need to leave."

"Patrick," Fredrick said from behind us. "Leave Abby alone. If she bought a ticket, then she has every right to be here."

"Fred, don't let her manipulate you," Patrick said.

"I expected her to be here. I'm ready for this," Fredrick said with a slow blink and a sigh.

"Fine, I wash my hands of this," Patrick said and wiped his hands together. "Come on, Emma. I think they're serving the meal."

I let Patrick lead me back to our table. I didn't hear anything Abby and Fredrick said to each other. Louisa, thankfully, missed all of it. We found her at the table eating the salad at her seat.

"Freddy went to the bathroom," Louisa said when she swallowed her bite.

"Louisa, I told you not to call him Freddy. His name is Fredrick. Please call people the name they want to be called," I said.

Chapter Twelve

We took the train from New York to Boston the following afternoon. It was a tense ride in first-class seating. We sat facing each other with a table between us. Patrick and Fredrick had window seats and spent the trip on their laptops. I spent most of the trip reading one of the books I had grabbed at PubCon. Only Louisa looked bored.

"Emma," Louisa said. "You must be so excited to show us Chicago. Freddy, did you know Emma went to Northwestern?"

"Actually, I do," Fredrick said without looking up from his laptop. "We knew each other our last two years there."

Louise was silent. I eventually looked up to see her wide-eyed, mouth opened, looking back and forth between us. "What!? Emma, you never told me you knew Freddy."

I sighed but looked back at my book. "I knew Fredrick while I was in Chicago," I said.

Louisa adjusted her position to turn toward Fredrick and leaned toward him, her hand on his arm. "OMG, Freddy, what was she like? What do you think of her since you last saw her? Was she cool? Did she party? Did she get DRUNK!? OMG! OMG! OMG! I have to tell Mary! Mary will die!"

Fredrick stopped typing and lowered his laptop screen before looking at her. "I'm not the best judge of cool, but I did see her get drunk a few times. She's still the same, but different. New York has changed her."

He turned to look at me, and our eyes locked.

Louisa didn't notice because she had turned to me as well. "How? She seems the same to me."

"There is a hardness I never noticed in Chicago. It's as if she's lost all sense of wonder and curiosity and joy in the world."

"Oh, that's just being a New Yorker," Louisa said, waving her hand and dismissing all of it.

"Then I'm glad I'm not a New Yorker," Fredrick said, not breaking eye contact.

I sat there, feeling uncomfortable as all three looked at me. "I have to pee," I said, putting my book aside and getting up.

When I slid the bathroom door behind me, I shut my eyes tight and rubbed my eyes. I could feel the tears building. I had said the first thing that popped into my head so I could get out of there. I was uncomfortable with the feelings this was bringing up, and I knew I was ready to cry. I gave myself two minutes to cry and regret everything. After that, I wiped my eyes, blew my nose, fixed my makeup, and went back to my seat.

Boston, DC, and Atlanta passed quickly without incident. Thanks to Patrick and Louisa, my involvement with Fredrick was kept to a minimum. I had a chance to spend time with people I knew in the area. I had done so many conferences and book tours that bookstore owners and managers had become my friends, even if we rarely saw each other. The East Coast was easy for me. I dreaded LA and Chicago, but Los Angeles was Fredrick's home. There were parties and events that Patrick insisted I attend.

"Look, I know you have the life you want in New York. I just feel like you owe it to yourself to see what life would have been like if you had made a different decision," Patrick said one night as we had dinner together in Atlanta without Louisa and Fredrick.

He had been trying to bring this up throughout the tour, and I had been redirecting conversations when it happened. There was no way to shift the conversation now.

"Do all his friends know about me?" I asked, bracing myself for the worst news possible.

Patrick gave me a dubious look. "Emma, he wrote a whole fucking movie about your break-up. They all think the worst of you."

"Did you?" I asked, bracing myself worse.

"Honestly, yes. I was expecting another Abby," he said with a grin. "I thought Louisa was you when I first met her."

I had to laugh because nobody had ever mistaken Louisa and me. "I never knew he had a type."

Patrick drank some wine as he considered his response. "I think he shifted his type because of you. It is like he started dating the anti-Emma. The difference is that these women make him miserable."

"He seems to like Louisa," I said with a shrug.

"Louisa is the anti-Emma too," Patrick added, tapping his finger on the table. "Come to the parties so you can at least enjoy the confusion when people first think Louisa is you and then have to do a double-take when they realize this tall, statuesque brunette is the real Emma."

I shook my head. "Then they'll just ignore me and leave me alone. I really don't like parties. The anchor thing you noticed at the first signing was something we did for each other. Book signings are where I am comfortable. Parties... not so much, especially when everyone already knows who I am and has judged me. Fredrick won't help me."

"Then I will. Plus, you can meet Victor, who has an ass that won't quit," Patrick said and winked.

I couldn't help but laugh. "He's not my type."

Patrick chuckled with me. "Oh, I know your type. Taller than you, a dork, who would rather be naked than in a tux, and no ass."

I felt myself blush. "He really looked good in that tux," I whispered.

Patrick raised an eyebrow. "I noticed you fixed his tie. Here's a secret. I saved it for you. I could've fixed it if I wanted. I thought to myself, Emma needs one little moment of happiness to get her through this tour."

"Happiness would be not being on tour," I said as my good mood sank.

Patrick patted my hand. "Emma, I figured you out the moment I met you. This tour will probably be the best thing that has ever happened to you. Trust me, next year you will call me and tell me exactly that. Come to the parties. If Fredrick doesn't anchor you, then I will. Now that I know you need it, I know what to do."

I smiled at him, again feeling overwhelmed by my long-repressed emotions. After dinner, as we walked through downtown Atlanta, Patrick stopped and wrapped his arms around me. I couldn't fight it anymore, and I cried in the arms of a man I barely knew. He didn't say anything. He just let me cry.

Chapter Thirteen

I sat on the aisle next to Louisa during the flight to LA. Thankfully we were in first class, and the drinks were free. I debated getting drunk on the flight. I decided against it, not sure what I would do once I was drunk. We both tried to sleep for a while. I put in my earbuds and listened to some soft music. I kept replaying my dinner with Patrick and the disastrous fantasies I had later that night when I thought about how Fredrick's friends would treat me. I repeatedly played through a scene where they all pointed and threw stones while laughing at me.

When I couldn't stand dwelling on that anymore, I switched to thinking about how my career seemed to be taking five steps back. I was supposed to be working with authors to create the best version of their books and publish them. Now I was babysitting a celebrity author, who also happened to be my ex, on his book tour with his publisher and an intern. I was the least helpful person and a waste of time and money for my employer. Clearly, I was in demand, and the time I spent here was time I wasn't working with other authors. The more I thought about what was going on, the less it made sense.

After mentally yelling at myself, I finally gave up on sleep and ordered a glass of wine.

"Can't sleep?" Louisa asked, pulling her eye mask off and pulling out her own earbuds.

I shook my head. "I'm ready for Cape Cod," I told her.

"The best I can offer right now is the beach in Los Angeles," she said with a bit of bounce.

I did my best to smile. Louisa looked out the window as the flight attendant brought my wine. I took a sip and let out a sigh.

"We're here to work," I reminded her.

"We should go to the beach one day, just you and me," Louisa said. "We aren't working twenty-four-seven. We can take a day off."

"Maybe," I said between sips of wine.

Louisa adjusted in her seat to face me. "What about tomorrow while they're doing the morning shows? We can get suntans before we get to Cape Cod! Everyone will be so jealous of our pre-vacation tans. Mary will demand to know why we left her behind. Then she'll complain for hours, and we'll giggle because we won, again."

I chuckled and shook my head. "It's not hard to make Mary jealous. We don't have to go out of our way to do so. Anyway, I have an appointment tomorrow morning."

"What appointment?" Patrick asked, sitting up and leaning into the aisle.

The one detail I had been keeping to myself since my conversation with Patrick. It was time to come clean. I didn't know who to trust anymore, but there was one person who would be honest with her, hoping that it would give him what he wanted. I took a sip of the wine to give me a moment to think of how to respond. "It's just with a friend who started his own publishing company in LA. He wants me to come by and see what he's done in the two years since they started."

"A job interview?" Patrick asked, leaning on the arm of his seat.

"No, I mean... yeah, sort of," I said, trying to explain why I would have this meeting when I didn't want to move to Los Angeles. "Technically. He keeps offering me a job, but I can't leave New York."

"So, you go to the interview, you lead him on, tease him a bit, and then say no when he offers you a job," Fredrick said from his seat.

I leaned forward and saw that he was staring at the back of his seat. "No, this is the first time I've ever come out," I said, wanting to clear up his confusion. "He was at Pub-Con and insisted I stop by when he heard I was going to be in Los Angeles. I decided to accept the meeting since I have the free time this week."

Fredrick turned his head and glared at me. I stopped talking about it at this point because I wasn't sure I was explaining it accurately or if Fredrick would understand. It was clear all he could see was a pattern. Nothing was going to make him see this any other way.

"Is it Ted?" Louisa asked. "Your dad is always complaining about Ted, the publisher in LA."

"Yes, it's Ted," I said, hoping explaining this to the men would help Fredrick understand. "Ted was my father's protege. When my father retired, he packed up and moved to Los Angeles. Ted thinks the West Coast needs more major publishers. He swears he needs me because authors will follow me to any publisher."

"Move it. I have to go to the bathroom," Fredrick said to Patrick.

As Fredrick got up and walked away, I could see the back of his neck getting redder.

"What's up with him?" Louisa asked.

The three of us watch Fredrick bang into some of the seats and swear.

"I think Fredrick had some type of epiphany. You know these creative types. Inspiration can come at any moment," Patrick said.

"He looked mad," Louisa added.

Patrick said nothing as he turned and met my eyes. I knew why Fredrick Wentworth was angry, and it was my fault. While Fredrick was in the bathroom, we all switched seats. I took the window seat, and Patrick took mine, putting Louisa happily next to Fredrick. I put on my headphones and closed my eyes. I was pretending to be asleep before Fredrick got back to his seat.

It was early afternoon when we landed in LA, so Louisa and I played tourist together. Patrick called and insisted we come to his home for a Fredrick-free dinner. As we walked around Beverly Hills, I kept reminding myself that I only had to get through a week in LA and three days in Chicago. Yes, these would be the two most difficult stops on tour. Once we got back to New York, I would be done and off to Cape Cod. After that, everything could get back to normal. The only thing I ended up buying was a simple bathing suit at Patrick's instruction. I hadn't planned to swim, but he insisted we would at dinner.

Louisa was excited to go, even if Fredrick wasn't there. Dinner was fantastic, and Victor was everything Patrick had promised. We got drunk, swam in the pool, and I felt like this was the first relaxing night I had had in months. Nobody mentioned Fredrick Wentworth or books. We talked about nothing and everything, played Cards Against Humanity (Patrick and I were declared the worst people in the world), and Louisa got to flirt with Seth, one of their friends.

Seth was an actor I had seen often playing the Asian friend in movies. He was half Korean with jet black hair and green eyes. He had just become the next hot thing when cast as one of the lead actors in Fredrick's newest sitcom project. The show was already getting a ton of positive buzz for its diversity both behind the scenes and on the screen.

"I think I like you more than I like Fredrick," Patrick said as we lounged next to the pool in the dark. We were very drunk.

"Thank you," I said with a giggle.

Patrick pulled out another bottle of wine and poured more into my glass. "I'm serious."

"So am I!"

"Then why did you turn down the proposal?"

I took a deep breath. I needed the air to clear out my head for this answer. Patrick, after all, only heard Fredrick's side of the story. "So many reasons."

"I refuse to believe that. I have figured you out already. You're a checklist type of woman. You had pros and cons. What were the cons? They obviously won."

I clinked my glass against his. "No publishing companies out here."

"That's not true anymore," Patrick said with a wave of his free hand.

"My family is all in NYC."

"From what Louisa says, they don't deserve you. You're a saint, and they're the sinners. These are lame cons."

"They weren't the deciding reasons. They were the whipped cream and cherry on top of the big one,"

Patrick rolled onto his side, spilling his wine a little. "Please tell me."

I hadn't talked about the real reasons with anyone after Karen, and I had made my pro/con list at graduation. It was enough that my family and job were in New York. Nobody ever wondered why I never sought more for myself.

I drank all the wine in my glass, hoping for the inhibition to be honest with Patrick and myself. "In the end, I didn't know if I loved him enough to give up everything that I wanted to move to a place where I had nobody and nothing," I said in one breath.

Patrick remained silent, not even moving to refill my wine. I took a deep breath and continued. "I firmly believed, at twenty-two, that I wasn't nor were our feelings strong enough for me to give up my career, leave my friends and family behind, and follow him. I honestly thought I would grow to resent him and stop loving him."

"He didn't agree," Patrick said, reminding me of what we both knew.

"It all seemed so easy to him. He had everything here. His friends would obviously be my friends. His family would be my family. I could just go to New York when I was needed. He was so positive, but it was easy for him. I could no more ask him to move to New York for me than agree to move to LA for him," I blurted out in one breath.

Patrick finally reached for the bottle of wine and refilled my glass. "Was it the right decision?"

"If you asked me that question last month, I would have said yes."

"Now?"

I didn't say anything for a few moments. I was lost replaying every glare and angry comment he had made since PubCon. "He doesn't feel the same, so it doesn't matter. Louisa is the type of woman he wants to be with, not me. I just make him angry."

"You two are so oblivious," Patrick said with a laugh.

"What does that mean?"

"Nothing."

Chapter Fourteen

I was left on my own now that we were in Los Angeles. Louisa, who had been so excited to spend time with me before we got here, was utterly infatuated with Seth and spent her free time with him. Patrick and Fredrick stayed at home, only going to events when needed. I found myself with free time to get other tasks done. I sat by the pool now that I had a bathing suit, read manuscripts, or checked emails. I had never been this involved with a tour, and I was falling behind on my own work.

I was exhausted from trying to hold everything together, but every night I was picked up by Patrick and Victor and taken to another party in honor of Fredrick and the book. We would get to the party, Fredrick would already be there, he would be drunk (or maybe high), and he would brood. Patrick would take me around and introduce me to people. I heard the same things repeatedly as people realized who I was.

"You're so not his type."

"That blond girl with Seth is much more Fredrick's type."

"You're nothing like he wrote you in the movie."

"Fuck me, you're hot."

That last one was from one of the biggest douchebags in all of Hollywood. He didn't even remember that, when he was trying to get a terrible memoir published a few years ago, he had flirted with me at a party in New York City. He had stalked me at said party until I left. He must have been too drunk to remember anything from that night, and I wondered if the same would happen again.

One of the most surreal moments at the party was when I met Sammy, the petite blonde actress who played me in Fredrick's first movie. Aside from that one role, I'm a huge fan, and we hit it off. We met at a small party of friends that the above-mentioned douchebag threw our second night in town. She and I sat in a quiet room with her sleeping baby.

"Is this as weird for you as it is for me?" Sammy asked when we were alone in the room.

I was happily bouncing the giggling child on my lap and making silly faces. "Why? Yes, but why?" I asked without looking away from the chubby baby.

Sammy shrugged. "I feel like I know who you are. We made some big changes to the character because I thought they were too unfair. I spent a lot of time trying to figure her out, and now that I know you, I think I really got in your head more than I realized."

That got me to look up. What little I had seen of the movie had hurt. I hadn't considered that this had been someone's interpretation of Fredrick's work or that it could have been more generous than he had initially written. "Did you always know she was based on a real woman?" I asked, lowering my voice.

Sammy gave me a half-smile. "Then? No. Since then, I realized that Fredrick writes best when processing something difficult. This book is his way of working through Abby."

I shook my head. That was impossible, and since Sammy knew my history with Fredrick, I could openly talk about it. "He wrote this book before I even met him. I was the first person to read and edit it. Most of my edits made it into the final book."

Sammy looked confused. "Really? I wonder what he wrote to deal with Abby then?"

I was curious about that too. She was right about how Fredrick coped. Considering what I could tell at the parties, he got drunk and high each night, so I didn't know if he had remembered his healthy coping mechanisms.

I saw Sammy again the next night with her husband and baby in tow. This was a party Fredrick's agent threw, and many important Hollywood people were there. I was more comfortable at this party since few of them had known who I was to Fredrick. Sammy and I continued to chat about nonsensical things like how we both love knitting, have the same taste in music, disagree on which animals are the cutest, and other silly things. At some point, her six-month-old was back in my arms, falling asleep on my lap.

"This is probably the cutest thing I have ever seen," Patrick said, walking by.

Since I met Sammy, Patrick had kept his distance. He had not played anchor for me at all that evening. That comment was the first thing he said to me since introducing me to Sammy, and I noticed a few people turn to look at us, including Fredrick.

"Do you have children?" Sammy asked me.

This was the topic we had avoided for two nights.

I let out a sigh. "No. My younger sister, Louisa's sister-in-law, has two little boys. The oldest is almost four. I adore them."

"Can I ask you something personal?" Sammy asked as she looked behind me.

"Ok," I said, feeling more comfortable with her than I had with anyone outside my family in years.

"Has there been anyone in your life since Fredrick?"

I looked up and quickly found Fredrick in the crowd. He was sitting alone by the bar with a beer in his hand. He was staring at me, but I couldn't read his expression. It took a fraction of a second for me to replay the disastrous dates I had been on in the first few years after returning to New York. There had been a few short relationships, but I grew less tolerant of them as time went on. In the past year, there hadn't been more than one or two dates that ended poorly. I always made the mistake of comparing men to Fredrick without realizing it. Thinking of them all at once made me remember how happy Fredrick and I had been together, and I felt the tidal wave of emotions start to rise again. I tried to blink back the tears that were beginning to fill my eyes, but I had to wipe them away.

"He may date a lot of famous women, but none of them have been what he wants," Sammy said.

"He has made it clear he doesn't want me anymore even if I wanted to get back together," I said and cleared my throat.

Sammy kept her voice low and leaned forward so only I could hear what she had to say. "When I was trying to get into character, I imagined I would regret the decision right away. That's how I played her."

I knew she was trying to clarify that she understood some of what I was feeling, but it triggered something defensively. "I was twenty-two years old. I have a father who still refuses to work through the grief of my mother's death. I wanted a career that I couldn't have in LA at that point. I made the best decision I could make."

I took a deep breath and hugged the baby closer, wondering for a moment about what my life could have been like if I had made a different choice. Sammy put her hand over mine and squeezed.

"I know you now. It sounds about right to me," she said with a small smile.

I spent the rest of the night dwelling on the idea of regret. I started playing back moments in the past eight years, trying to imagine if it could have been different.

"Louisa, do you regret anything in your life?" I asked her on the ride back to the hotel after that party.

Louisa had decided to take the car back to the hotel with me. Seth looked crushed, but I noticed her give him her hotel room key card before he left.

"No!" she said with her usual peppiness.

"Why not?" I asked and turned to look at her.

Louisa shrugged and gave me a smile. "I'm sure I've made plenty of bad decisions, but I love who I am right now. If I regretted my mistakes or wished to change them, then I wouldn't be as awesome as I am."

I let out a small chuckle and found her positivity infectious for a moment before I remembered the regrets I had been ignoring for eight years. "What about when you don't like who you are?"

Louisa's smile dropped, and she got serious. She could tell there was something else going on, and I appreciated that she wasn't pushing me for more information. "I always know I'm in control of how awesome I am. If I make a wrong decision, I don't regret it. I just change things. It's never too late to change things, Emma."

I sat there for a moment, hoping she never became as cynical as I was. We were both wealthy, white, educated women. Louisa had no fear because the world had never been cruel to her. When I was her age, I had already lost my mother to cancer and my father to his grief. I was a lot like her when I had been at college, but returning to New

York changed me. Yes, I had the career I dreamed of, but I was starting to realize that I wasn't in as much control of that as I thought. Karen still had a heavy hand in my career, and something was going on with the company executives that I didn't understand yet. Would I have turned down the chance to be Fredrick's editor if the decision had been mine to make? I kept coming back to Karen's choices and their impact on my career.

I couldn't sleep that night as these thoughts went through my mind. How many books had Karen turned down even though I disagreed vocally? How many of those books had been major best sellers and award winners for other publishers? I remembered a rumor about how Karen was why Scholastic had published the US versions of Harry Potter. She had turned down the opportunity for us to publish it. Was she capable of making the best decisions for my career? Had I only trusted her because she had taken my parent's place in my life? I kept trying to imagine what life would have been like in LA if I had accepted Fredrick's proposal. I couldn't see it happening any other way. Yes, I like many of his friends now that I have met them. How many of these people would be in his life if he wasn't who he had become after our breakup? Would I hate being so far away from Mary and her family? I love my nephews and, when she is not desperate for attention, Mary is my best friend. Except not really. I had told Patrick more about myself in three weeks than I had ever told Mary.

Chapter Fifteen

I had been resisting visiting Ted's offices for years. He had been trying to entice me to take a job since he started the company. When I woke up the next morning for my meeting with Ted, I was convinced that he was the one person who could help me understand what was going on.

"EMMA!" Ted said as he gave me a huge hug and squeezed tight.

This was the man who had watched me grow up. He had a love/hate relationship with my father, but it had made them a powerhouse team. I was in a unique position to understand all the people around me and the business we worked in.

We started with a tour of his small suite of offices, and he introduced me to his staff. He showed me the books they had been publishing. The space was small and bustling. Walls were covered in bookshelves, and all shelves were filled with books. People's cubicles were piled high with manuscripts and posters of cover artwork leaned against walls. They struggled to find quality books to publish, but they clearly got many submissions. None of his editors had any solid contacts. They were limited to manuscripts sent to them. In most publishing companies, submissions are ninety percent crap. The agents bring the best authors, but they go to the companies they have relationships with. As we walked around, I found myself spinning ideas through my head about the type of help they needed and what I would do if I worked here. It had been a long time since I had felt this excited and energized.

After our tour, we went back to his office, and he closed the door behind him. I knew Ted was trying to entice me to work here and help him. It was evident in the way he talked about the business.

"I'm delighted I finally got you to come out here. I'm going to be honest with you, Emma, I need you here. You need to come out here and work with me," he said as he collapsed at his desk.

The small office he was using was much like the rest of the office. There were stacks of books scattered all over the office, most of them from his days in New York with my father. His desk and chairs were the ones he had taken from the office in New York when he moved out here.

I was torn in my desire to treat this as an information-gathering session and an actual interview. I couldn't ignore what was happening around me in New York and how different I felt on this tour.

I decided to be honest with him. If he was doing the hard sell, I would give him the harshest reality. "I wouldn't bring any authors with me, Ted."

I felt a little guilty about not mentioning that Tom Scott already promised to follow me anywhere I went and that other authors seemed to think I was leaving. I knew I could help him if I wanted to accept his offer. Even if I couldn't bring authors with me, I had enough contacts to get new ones into this company.

Ted waved his hand, dismissing my honesty. "I'll address that in a second, but let me tell you what I see happening in our industry. Publishing has always been based in New York. This will not change, but now smaller publishers are cropping up outside of New York. How many independent and small publishers showed up at PubCon this year?"

I thought about the exhibit floor this year. "The number seems to be growing," I said with a smile.

"Right," he said and extended a hand to display the piles of books around him, "but they rarely give books away to people. Maybe they will give two or three books away in limited numbers. They can't compete with the big guys because of the expense of just going to PubCon."

I shook my head, knowing he was right. Even when I walked past those booths, I was careful to only take books I wanted because I knew it was so expensive and I wasn't their target.

Ted continued, holding up a finger. "After what happened with the last day when the public attended, fewer indie publishers will come in the future. There's no way we could have stayed to give copies away to the public, on top of the industry insiders. The PubCon organizers knew that we could barely afford to attend as is. They wanted something more like a San Diego Comic-Con without proper planning. I hope Christi gets a shit-ton of money from them," he said and slapped his hand on his desk.

"I am sure they will learn from their mistake," I said as I sighed, not sure they would. "But this is all about money."

Ted nodded. It was something we both knew perfectly well. "A few of us smaller publishers have been talking. The bigger cities are doing more annual book fairs like Miami has done for years. Why can't we do that in different cities if PubCon shifts from an industry conference to a public event? Why not on another coast? New York does a Comic-Con that gets almost as many people as San Diego, but it doesn't diminish how large San Diego's is. What if we could pull in the tiny graphic novel publishers, all the special presses out here, and maybe even get the big New York City companies to attend? Think of all those who don't go to PubCon because of the travel: librarians, bloggers, bookstore owners, celebrities who want to write books, and more!"

His energy was infectious, but I forced myself to think clearly about this. If an event was planned from the ground up, that could work. "That's a great vision, but I can't help with that," I reminded him. "I might be great at planning a book tour, but I don't think I could take on a large convention."

Ted shook his head. "I need you here. I need your help with the authors we have. I just want you to see that publishing isn't all in New York anymore. It can happen anywhere. Plus, I hear the rumors. People will follow you when their contracts are complete."

Ted had opened the exact door I was hoping he would. "Sure, people would follow me eventually, but not many and not the big names," I reminded him.

"I know what people are saying. Tom Scott is almost done with his contract and told me he wants to work with you. Layla Dryfuse wants to bring both her academic and fiction books to the same publisher," Ted said, mentioning the authors I suspected he was speaking to.

Layla Dryfuse had been a friend of my mother. She had lived in New York with her chef husband until he burnt out, and they moved their family to Boston. Their kids were about a decade younger than me, but I remembered spending time with them when we were kids. She wrote academic work but had a pen name for her fiction. No other publisher was in a position to manage all her books, but Ted may be in a unique position to do just that.

While I was thinking, Ted continued. "I know that authors and agents are anxious they will be assigned to another editor and write details in their contracts that allow them to break the contract if you leave or another editor is assigned."

"How do you know about that?" I asked, wondering how many authors and agents had been denied access to me.

Ted put his hands up, hoping to ease my anxiety. "It's not something I have ever heard of people doing before, but that's how much people like working with you. Then there's something I heard about this book tour you're on. I know you're here because Christi got hurt, but there is a rumor you secretly edited Fredrick's novel. Do you know this?"

I was shocked, and I'm sure Ted could tell. My defensiveness rose, and my head was spinning with how little I knew. "First," I said, "maybe two authors have asked for that contract detail. It's not an epidemic, and those contracts have been signed recently. There has been no investment in those books yet. Don't count on that as a way to build your company around me. I have fifteen other authors who don't have that in a contract."

Ted pushed a box of tissues to me, and I took a breath. If anger was the only emotion I allowed myself to feel, then all the feelings were going to come out.

I took a tissue and wiped my eyes. "Second, and as far as Fredrick's novel goes, I happened to edit it years ago when we were at Northwestern together. We knew each other, I edited that literary journal, and he asked me to read it. How does anyone know that?"

"From what I overheard from your own colleagues at PubCon, his manuscript still had your notes on it," Ted said in a low voice.

That was the last thing I was expecting to learn. I thought back to Christi's interactions with me at PubCon. I hadn't recognized her snippy and territorial behavior at the time. I hadn't even registered it. That would explain some of why I was the one on this tour.

Ted narrowed his eyes and waited for me to respond. I remembered I wasn't really here for a job interview, no matter how I had tried to frame or pretend it was. I was here for advice from someone outside of my bubble. I was here to see a man who had been part of my life since I was born.

"I don't understand anything anymore," I whispered and took another tissue to blow my nose. "My career is stuck, I feel like this assignment is a punishment, and these weird rumors are spreading. Karen's no help anymore, and my father's in a tailspin."

"You can't carry the weight of all this responsibility, Emma. Your father and Karen are adults. I know she doesn't want to lose you, and I don't blame her, but you're an editor running the book tour for a man you rejected eight years ago."

"How do you know that I rejected him?" I abruptly interjected.

He raised his eyebrow and tilted his head to the side. "Your father told me."

Ted got up, sat in the chair next to mine, and wrapped his arm around my shoulder. I was surprised anything about Fredrick had registered for my father. For the first time in years, someone who has always loved me was available to comfort me instead of focusing on their own needs.

"If the rumors are true," Ted said as we sat together, "Karen cost the company some big titles and is on thin ice with the executives. She's keeping you close to cover her ass. You should be leading a team of editors. You should be running your father's imprint already. The story going around, directly from Fredrick's agent, is that they wanted you to be his editor, especially since you had already worked on it. Karen refused to let them even talk to you and sent them to Christi."

My mind was spinning but so much made sense if this was true. What shocked me was that Fredrick had wanted to work with me on this book. It would have been easy for him to run through the manuscript to make the corrections I suggested before sending it to agents. I wanted to know why but that would require talking to Fredrick about it. I was afraid he did it to make me uncomfortable. Had he insisted I travel on the tour with him when the opportunity came up? I couldn't think about it until I processed what Ted was saying about Karen and what it meant for my future in publishing.

"You make it sound like she is deliberately holding me back," I said as I lifted my head from his shoulder and wiped a tissue over my face.

"Oh, dear girl, no. I am sorry, I didn't mean it like that," Ted said and patted my hand. "She can't let you go because of your mother. She really thinks she is doing the best thing for you. That this is what your mother would have wanted. She means well, but you're thirty years old. Your mother wouldn't want you to be living like this. From the way your father talks, nothing has changed in your life since you came home from Chicago. You deserve so much more. Come here, work with me, be my partner, and we can make this company as big as Scholastic, Random House, and all the others. We could even be bigger than your father and I were in our heyday. Plus, you can bring anyone you want with you. My team needs new blood and a kick in the pants."

I couldn't say yes. There was too much information I needed to process and an author I still needed to babysit.

Chapter Sixteen

O ur last night in Los Angeles was spent at a small dinner party at Patrick's house. Fredrick was there this time, as were some of his closest friends, specifically those who had gotten along with me. Dinner was enjoyable, but I was anxious to get to Chicago and finish the tour. After Chicago, we would go home, and I would be done. Christi had emailed me to let me know she was ready to take on the last leg of the tour. Patrick pulled me aside after dinner to talk about Chicago.

"I'm not going," he said when I asked him what he knew of the morning shows.

I was confused but smiled. "Not going to the morning shows? Louisa did a good job here, so I am sure she can take over. She could do a book tour in her sleep now."

Patrick shook his head. "No, sweetie, I'm not going to Chicago. I was never going back to New York anyway, and you and Fredrick will be fine. Louisa can take on the morning shows so you can focus on the bookstores and parties. Everything is smooth sailing from here on out."

My smile fell. "There are no parties in Chicago."

"Perfect!" Patrick said, taking my hand to give me a high-five.

"Why aren't you coming? You're the only thing keeping me sane," I asked, pulling my hand out of his.

"I have a couple reasons. First, I need to get back to other clients. Second, I miss my bed so much, and I don't like hotel rooms. Third, I think you and Fredrick need to have some insanity. My presence has allowed the two of you to just avoid each other. Louisa can do what I've been doing. There are too many of us trying to do the job that only one needs to do. We know you can't leave, so I'm stepping out."

I could feel the panic filling my mind. "Fredrick doesn't want me around, I don't want to be around, and you've kept us from killing each other."

Patrick put his arm around my shoulder. "Emma, I don't know if you noticed, but you two are having a passive-aggressive-off."

"What does that mean?"

"You're brooding, moping, and constantly emotionally overwhelmed. This is not healthy for anyone. He's doing that too, but with pot and beer. You should just fuck and get it over with."

My eyes got wide. "What!?"

Patrick waved his hand. "Forget I said that. Have a fight, for fuck's sake. Talk to each other. You've barely said two words to each other all month. Louisa and I play go-between. You just have to get through a few more days in

Chicago, and then you can forget this entire month ever took place. Louisa said you're going to Cape Cod with your father and sister. That should be lovely. Oh, but Seth has decided to go to Chicago and New York with you. All the tickets and stuff were already paid for. Louisa and Seth are clearly head-over-heels in love. I'm not sure if you noticed."

I had noticed. I wondered what Louisa would do when put in the same situation as I had been.

Seth insisted on sitting next to Louisa on the flight to Chicago the next day. His excuse for joining us was that he and Fredrick needed to work on the sitcom scripts.

"Fredrick is letting Seth write with him," Louisa whispered to me as we sat at the gate. "They worked on the script for a movie together once, and Fredrick feels the script and acting will be stronger if Seth does both."

I was impressed with how Seth had found a great excuse so he could spend more time with Louisa. Still, this decision left me sitting next to Fredrick for the entire flight. As we sat there in awkward silence, I realized that Patrick had been right about how little Fredrick and I had spoken to each other this past month.

I tried to pretend I wasn't sitting next to the man I had loved. I sat with my arms close to my body, worried that our arms would brush. I pulled out my tablet and tried to read through a manuscript, but my mind kept replaying everything I had learned during my meeting with

Ted. The more I thought about it, the more frustrated I became. As confused as I was about what had happened with Fredrick's manuscript, I could see all the ways Karen had been holding me back.

I wasn't angry with her but with myself for allowing this to continue. Over the years, I had gone on autopilot at work. I had stopped pushing for more responsibility. I had let my responsibility for my father and Elizabeth take over my life, and everything else suffered as a result. I needed to regain control at work to do the work I wanted.

"So..." Fredrick said once the plane was in the air, pulling me out of my thoughts.

I looked across the aisle to Louisa for support, but she and Seth were already deep in their own conversation. I took a sip of champagne and told the worst story of my life.

"So, this morning when Louisa and I checked out, we were standing at the elevator, and we could hear the couple in the closest room having sex. They were both moaning quite loudly," I said.

I regretted the story immediately. There were so many other things I needed to talk to him about, and I had picked that. Fredrick looked at me like I was insane and turned toward the window. As I was about to put my earbuds in, I heard him chuckle to himself. I hoped it was the story that had amused him and not my stupidity.

Chapter Seventeen

I hadn't been in Chicago since graduation. After I left, I had put away my happy memories. I had spent the last eight years trying to forget how happy I had been with Fredrick. I could not ignore the returning memories as we drove through the city to the hotel. I listened to Louisa prattle on about Navy Pier, pizza, shopping, weird sculptures, and all the other things she wanted to see.

"Are you guys going to visit old haunts?" Louisa asked Fredrick and me.

The two of us just stared at her.

"You two are officially the worst. Here we are, in a city you both spent four years in. Who better to suggest good restaurants and things to do? It's like the two of you exist on separate planes of existence where you don't even realize the other is there. Emma, have you met Freddy? Freddy, have you met Emma?"

"Louisa, his name is Fredrick, not Freddy. Has anyone else called him Freddy?" I said.

"I heard you call him Freddy at the library in New York."

I wanted to justify why, but I said nothing because I knew I couldn't say anything without getting over-whelmed with emotions. Even without that conversation, I could feel my eyes fill with tears.

"Jesus, Emma. What is going on with you?" Louisa asked.

She sounded annoyed.

"I'm just ready to go home. I'm ready to get back to my life," I said, wiping my eyes.

I decided to create a plan to regain control of my career and life. I spent the evening in my hotel room, putting all the pieces together. Karen's control of my career had started at graduation when she had persuaded me to refuse Fredrick. The week we spent in Los Angeles made me see that I could have a life there, but I still felt, at twenty-two, it wouldn't have worked. So much of my world had changed in these eight years that I could make that change now. I wasn't sure I wanted it.

Yes, I was still in love with Fredrick. That was clear after these past few weeks. I spent the last eight years lying to myself to just get through life without him. Accepting this reality had been like removing a dam from a river. The emotions just flowed out of me now. I desperately wanted Fredrick to knock on my door and kiss me. I repeatedly played the fantasy in my head, making it difficult to focus on my career plans. I got a few plans in place before I gave up and asked Louisa to meet me in the lobby so we could discuss the remaining events.

"I appreciate the work you've been doing during this tour," I told her, wanting to make sure Louisa knew she was much more than a glorified babysitter.

"It's been a learning experience," she said with a big smile on her face.

"I need you to keep building on what you've learned, especially without Patrick here to help," I said and looked around to make sure Fredrick wasn't around. "This will be an experience no other intern will have. It will look good on your resume. I want you to work for me when the summer's over. Is that something you'd be interested in?"

Louisa's smile faded. "Will you be able to hire anyone?" she asked.

That surprised me. From all that was happening to me, I didn't feel that my job was on the line. I assumed the executives were pissed at Karen, but maybe my career depended on hers more than I realized.

I thought about my response for a moment. "If I go somewhere else, would you want to come with me?"

Again Louisa's reaction confused me as she narrowed her eyes and pursed her lips. This was not the flighty Louisa I had known for decades. This was a woman who was seriously considering her future.

"Like LA?" she asked.

I shrugged, "Possibly."

"I don't want to be an editor. I wanted to do publicity, marketing, and public relations. I like this work a lot more than reading and editing books," she said, sitting back.

I nodded. "That's good to know."

"I'm not saying yes," Louisa added in a low voice. "I prefer working with you than Christi. You keep a level head even when you're not in control."

I locked eyes with her. "Take the lead tomorrow if you want to show the executives that you should be given a job. I'll make sure they know how you could have done this without me."

Her eyes got wide. "Then you might get fired!"

I smiled. "I'm willing to take that chance. You've got this."

I stayed in the hotel room watching Fredrick on the scheduled local morning shows. I felt more relaxed than I had all tour until I got to the first bookstore we were visiting in Chicago: the Northwestern University bookstore. Once everything was set up to my liking, I found Fredrick, Louisa, and Seth in the break room, waiting for the reading to start. My anxiety wasn't about the reading but being around Fredrick now that I could admit I was still in love with him.

"Coffee? Tea?" I asked.

"Beer," Fredrick said.

"No," I said, putting my finger on my lip. "I'll just go and get us tea."

When I returned with the tea and coffee (and water for Seth), I found Fredrick pacing. I had never seen him do this before because Patrick usually stayed with Fredrick before the reading.

"Emma," Louisa said, glancing at Fredrick. "What was that little chant you said when you walked out of the room?"

I knit my eyebrows together. "What do you mean? What little chant?"

"Cup, cup, cup, cup, tea, tea, tea, tea," she said with a half-smile.

I laughed a little to myself. I'd been doing that for so long that I no longer realized I did it. "My mother used to say that when she made me a cup of tea. You should know where it's from. You've seen the movie plenty of times."

"I have no idea," Louisa said, shaking her head.

"My Fair Lady," Fredrick said as he paced.

Louisa looked back and forth between the two of us. "Ok, so the two of you obviously know this, and I have no memory of that line from the movie. I've been watching you all month, and you say it every time you go get drinks."

I looked at Fredrick, expecting him to relax or catch my eye, but he continued pacing. "It's from when Eliza is learning to speak better," I said. "He makes her say 'cup of tea' over and over. She keeps saying cuppa tea, which most British people actually say."

"Yeah, I don't care. What I find amusing," Louisa said. "Every time you say it, Freddy mouths it along with you in perfect time and then laughs to himself."

I over at Fredrick again, but his back was to me, and he was looking over the passage he would read. He had probably heard me say it so many times while we were together that it was just stuck in his head.

Louisa looked playfully annoyed. "Is it a Northwestern thing? A Chicago thing? Freddy does it every time. EVERY TIME!"

"Does it annoy you?" Seth asked, a big grin on his face.

"No, but it makes me feel like there's some inside joke that I don't get! It makes me feel like Mary, and I hate that," Louisa said, turning to me.

"It's really nothing," Fredrick said as I gave Louisa a half-smile.

I wasn't going to blurt out our history without his consent. Louisa reluctantly let it drop.

The next day Louisa had asked for the afternoon off to spend it with Seth. I couldn't deny her some free time after doing so much the day before. I went to Fredrick's room to go to the next bookstore together. I thought it would be fine since nothing had gone wrong yet. When Fredrick opened the door and saw me standing there, rather than Louisa, I realized that nobody had told him about the change.

"Where's Louisa?" Fredrick said, looking behind me.

I tried to act casual about her absence. "She asked for the afternoon off."

"And you said yes?" Fredrick asked, his jaw getting tense as his mouth tightened. "She was the last thing keeping this from being the worst tour in the history of tours."

"Excuse me?" I said, rapidly blinking.

I wasn't expecting this reaction after things had been so calm all tour.

Fredrick filled up the doorway and leaned forward. "Christi assured me you were the best at running book tours, but this has been the worst experience of my life. I pity the other authors you work with and everyone else if this is your best."

I wasn't going to let him try to intimidate me, so I stood straight and took a step forward. "Maybe if you could avoid getting drunk and high, you would see that this tour is fantastic. You're already on the top of the New York Times bestseller list. We had to ship extra books to the bookstores, and that's still not enough. They're getting a second printing going earlier than expected because this tour has gone so well."

He didn't back down. "The tour is about me, and I'm not happy."

The look on his face was like one I often saw on my nephews when they were stubbornly refusing to do something asked of them. I could feel the heat rise in my face.

"The tour is about your fucking book," I said and took another step forward, hoping to push my way into his room so we didn't have this fight in the hall, but he wouldn't budge. "None of this is about you beyond the fact that you wrote the book. I'm here to make sure the investment was worth it for my bosses. I'm here because they don't trust anyone else to do this."

"Except you pass things off to Louisa and Patrick."

"You have made it clear that you don't want to interact with me. You asked Patrick to protect you from your big bad ex-girlfriend. He and I assumed you would be happier if he supported you."

Fredrick took a step out of his room, closer to me. "Yeah, and it has all fallen apart since he left."

"Sorry, you aren't as mature as he thinks you are. He thought you could handle another few days with me. What did you expect would happen after eight years? Do you think this is easy for me?"

"It was easy enough for you to walk away and say no eight years ago. I thought you wouldn't have a problem doing it this time."

We were standing inches from each other. I fought my instinct to kiss him.

"You want to see a clusterfuck? I will give you a clusterfuck," I said and took a step back. "The limo is waiting for you to take you to the bookstore. Feel free to tell the manager you fired me."

I turned and walked down the hall.

I would like to stay. I stubbornly stuck to that. I would like to say it was a disaster. I didn't, and it wasn't. I let him panic, but in reality, I was fifteen minutes behind him and on the phone with the manager before either of us got to the bookstore. I even relayed a message to Fredrick through the manager.

"You really want me to use the word fuck?" the manager said on the phone.

"You can say you are simply quoting me: get your own fucking cup cup cup cup of tea tea tea tea."

"He'll understand?"

"Oh, don't worry about that," I said as I mentally prepared a text to Patrick.

"Are you sure?"

"Totally."

"He won't get angry?" the manager asked, and I could hear the hesitancy in his voice.

"He's already angry. He thinks he fired me."

"He can't, right? You're on your way? Promise me you're on your way, Emma."

I smiled, confident that this would work out as I anticipated. "I promise, I'm on my way. He just won't know I am."

He had no idea I was there. I know because he told me at dinner that night.

Louisa insisted I meet her and Fredrick for dinner at the hotel dining room. I found her sitting at a booth in the back, snarling. I had let Fredrick push my buttons, and my reaction had been immature.

"I don't know why the two of you seem to hate each other, but I don't care," Louisa said when we were both at the table, sitting next to each other. "Clearly, this is something that happened years ago, before this book tour. We only have two more days together, and I am demanding you call a cease-fire."

She looked like she was ready for a night on the town. She was dressed in a short, sparkly dress with silver sandals. This was the first time her shoes actually seemed appropriate for the outfit. Her hair and makeup were perfect. She and Seth were probably planning a night out together. I, meanwhile, was dressed in jeans and a ratty t-shirt. Fredrick wore something similar and looked exhausted. Most authors looked like this towards the end of a book tour. This was the closest he and I had been in years, and there was no armrest between us like on the plane.

"She left me alone at the bookstore," Fredrick said, turning to glare at me.

"You fired me!"

"I got your message. I can get my own fucking glass glass glass glass of scotch scotch scotch scotch too," he said and tried to catch a waiter.

"Well, you're thirty years old. I should hope so," I said under my breath.

"I did my own reading too, and it was the best one of this whole tour."

"You idiot, I was there."

"HA! I thought I saw you in the back."

"You don't get it. This is not about you. It's about the book. You can't fire me any more than I could say no when I was told to do this tour."

"Enough!" Louisa said. "For the last month, the two of you couldn't be bothered to say anything to each other. Now you're fighting like you have been married as long as my parents."

That was the comment that shut us both up.

Chapter Eighteen

The day had gone well, and the tour was over. Louisa decided to manage the last day in Chicago. She may not have understood why, but she could tell I needed more of a break than I had asked for. I spent the next day relaxing at the hotel, but Louisa refused to let me spend the last night alone in my room. After dinner, the four of us walked around Navy Pier. It was a rainy and windy night, but Louisa was in a wonderful mood. Plus, it was pretty clear that Louisa was in love with Seth.

"You can call yourself the Princess of Book Tours," I said after she told me about the bookstore signing.

"Someday, I will take the title of Queen from you!"

"You can have it," I said with a sigh. "I'm just really good at planning book tours, but I hate doing events. They're perfect to do when you're young."

"Emma, you're thirty, not dead," Louisa said with a giggle. "Mary would die to go on a tour like this. I bet even Elizabeth would jump at the chance."

I rolled my eyes and giggled. "Elizabeth would never come. It would be work, and we both know Elizabeth is allergic to work."

Fredrick and I had gone back to ignoring each other. We walked around for a few hours letting the rain fall on us. Louisa wanted to be on the water, next to the water, or near the water. She wanted to enjoy her last night in Chicago with her favorite people. Fredrick kept up with Louisa, but Seth lingered behind with me.

"I think I am in love with her," Seth confessed after a while.

"With Louisa, what you see is what you get," I said with a smile. "If you know you love her like this, then you probably are."

"I came to Chicago, so I could spend time with her," he said, but he wasn't smiling. I could see the panic on his face. "In LA, she didn't seem this absorbed with Fredrick. I'm worried and don't know what to do."

I was sure Louisa had told him that we were more than colleagues. I understood he wanted help from me, who knew Louisa like a sister. "I wish I could tell you where her heart lies, but I'm too self-absorbed right now," I said, wishing I could give him more insight.

He looked down as we walked. "I haven't told her why you and Fredrick are so angry with each other. She's really frustrated with the two of you and a bit angry that I won't talk about it."

"Patrick told me you came to spend time with her. If she doesn't know that, what have you been telling her? Why does she think you came with us?"

"Oh, she thinks I'm here to work on scripts with Fredrick. I mean, we are working, but I don't really care that much about the show anymore. When she and I go out together, we have a great time. I think we are connecting. I would leave LA and move to New York to be with her. Then Fredrick's around, and she's completely focused on him."

There was a gust of wind that nearly blew us over. Then we heard Louisa scream and the thunk of her head hitting the ground.

Fredrick said she had been dancing along a low, stone wall. He was trying to get her down, but she was stubborn and insisted she could walk on her own. She had no idea how windy it gets in Chicago, and she was a little drunk. There had been a lot of wine at dinner. The combination of the wet stones, an impaired mind, and a burst of strong wind hit her at the wrong moment. She lost her footing and fell. She wasn't responding, and I refused to let anyone move her. I was afraid she had injured her back. The ambulance was there in less than a minute after I called them. Fredrick and Seth fought over who would ride with her. While they fought, I got in the back of the ambulance and yelled the name of the hospital to the men.

"Follow us!" I said before the paramedic closed the doors and drove off.

I was on the phone with the Musgroves as we drove to the hospital. They insisted they would be there in a few hours. I called Karen at home and told her what had happened. Technically we were on work time even though we weren't working. I didn't know if there would be legal action, but I wanted to cover my bases. She told me to have everyone write down what happened and email their comments to her. She would deal with it in the morning.

At the hospital, I was told to sit in the waiting room. While I waited, I typed out my account on my iPad. I told Fredrick and Seth to do the same before I emailed them all to Karen.

"You're always so calm under pressure," Fredrick said, sitting down next to me.

He slumped in the chair from physical and emotional exhaustion.

"Someone has to be," I said as I composed an email to Christi letting her know about the accident.

"You knew exactly what to do."

I didn't look up but gave him a half-shrug. "First aid certification, Girl Scouts, lifeguarding, and my father."

"You're the type of person who would get first aid training just in case you need it someday."

I didn't know what to say to that but realized I needed to give him my full attention at the moment.

"I'm sorry about what I said yesterday," he said when I met his eyes. "This tour hasn't been that bad. Considering our history, which apparently nobody has told Louisa about, you've been amazing. Did you call her parents?"

"They should be here soon, and nobody in my world knows about our history," I said, bracing myself for a fight.

Fredrick looked at me and rubbed his eyes. "Seth said he's staying with her. Even if she wakes up, they won't let her fly for a few days. It will be just you and me on the flight back to New York."

"I assumed so," I said as my phone rang. "Don't worry, you don't have to talk to me."

It was Christi on the phone, and I walked away to take it in private.

"Is she ok?" Christi asked when I told her everything. "This book tour is cursed!"

I chuckled to myself. "This is why editors don't go on book tours!"

Christi giggled a little. "Now we have leverage the next time they demand one of us go with an author."

"I have to tell you something," I said, realizing this was my chance to clear the air. "I didn't know something until recently, and you deserve honesty."

Christi didn't respond for a few seconds. "Ok," she said, drawing out the word.

"I was friends with Fredrick in college," I said as I let out a deep breath. "I edited this book nearly a decade ago, and I believe the draft they submitted still had my notes on it."

There was silence on the other end of the call. "Why did you refuse to be his editor? He sent it to your imprint first," Christi finally said.

"I didn't refuse it. I didn't even know about it until you accepted it. I'm not sure about what happened, but I think my notes seemed to cause some of the problems we're both facing."

"Would you have given him a contract if you had read it?" she asked.

I had to think about that one. "No," I said, "but I would have been open about giving it to someone I trust, like you."

Christi was silent again, and I let her think about her response. "You need to be careful," she blurted out. "From the meetings I've been part of, I can tell they are looking for an excuse to fire Karen, and they think you're making the same mistakes."

"I appreciate you telling me that. I wish it had never gotten this bad."

"Me too," she said before we got off the phone.

The Musgroves arrived just before Louisa woke up. As expected, they would not allow her to fly back to New York the next day. There was nothing wrong with her, but they wanted to watch her in case of a concussion. Her parents were just happy she was unhurt. They hugged all of us. When she insisted that Seth stay with her, I knew he didn't have to worry about Louisa's feelings anymore. The look on her face said it all. She had no interest in Fredrick. She was as in love with Seth as he was with her. The Musgroves saw it too and were happy to include Seth in their plans.

Fredrick and I were left on our own to fly back to New York. We were too exhausted to fight anymore. I fell asleep as soon as the plane took off and didn't wake up until it landed. When we arrived at Fredrick's New York hotel, Christi was there to greet us.

"Thank you for everything these past few weeks," Fredrick said before I left.

I think I said, "You're welcome."

I spent my first night home in bed, asleep. I allowed myself to release all the emotion I had denied myself for eight years and one month. I called in sick to work the next day even though I was slightly worried about how this would look. I had been focused on taking control of my professional life. I needed to do the same with my personal life. I may not have a chance with Fredrick, but that didn't mean I needed to ignore those memories. I looked around my apartment, and nothing seemed right. I pulled out boxes of pictures from my four years in Chicago, hoping to find an easy solution as I had for work. Looking at the photos, the knick-knacks, and love letters just made me want to cry. I couldn't just put these old things into my current life. It all seemed wrong. I had been ignoring my happiness for so long that I worried I needed a complete reboot.

Chapter Nineteen

I didn't go back to the office before leaving for my Cape Cod vacation. Other than the group still in Chicago, everyone was already there. Elizabeth and my father were settled in our cottage, which had been in my mother's family for generations. My family didn't know that I rented it out in the winter as a writer's retreat. The money went into my father's trust to create a little cushion. I suspected neither my father nor Elizabeth would curb their spending enough to make this unnecessary. I was trying to prevent a real crisis.

I wish I could say that Elizabeth and my father were happy to see me when I arrived, but they weren't. Neither asked how the book tour or PubCon had been. They were too busy going to parties and clam bakes and whatever it was that kept my sister out all night. A part of me hoped Elizabeth's absences were because she was working a secret job. I had a little fantasy that it was something she wouldn't want us to know about and maybe illegal. I just wanted her to be doing something with her life.

My first stop, after unpacking, was to walk over to see my friend Penny Smith. Penny had gone to Northwestern with me and knew Fredrick. She had spent plenty of time with him in the two years he and I had dated. Penny now lived in a small apartment behind an ice cream shop away from the beach. Years ago, she had been in a car accident and lost the use of her legs. Since then, she has become a huge activist for the disabled. She was often asked to speak at conferences, testify to Congress, appear at rallies, and do all sorts of things. She traveled all over the world. She often told me her life hadn't begun until she thought it was over. The last time I had seen her, the year before, she had finished her Ph.D. and decided to write a memoir that I wanted to publish. I had spent many Skype conversations trying to get her to sign a contract. She refused for, what she claimed, were personal objections to my bosses. She thought I worked for jackasses.

"I want to know everything. Please tell me you slept with him," Penny said as her nurse/assistant let me into the apartment.

"Who?" I asked, pretending I was oblivious.

"Fredrick!"

I rolled my eyes. "No, we barely spoke except one day in Chicago when we fought."

She took my hand and squeezed it. "Oh, Emma."

This was when I told her everything that had happened over the past month, including the political games his book had started in the office.

"This is a breakthrough," Penny said when I was done.

"It just feels like a breakdown," I said, feeling just as exhausted as I had been through the tour.

"Nothing is ever broken, Emma." She reminded me with a gesture to her legs. "Now that you've admitted how you feel, you can finally work through it. This is grief, and you know how to pull through that."

"I need a distraction," I said with a wave of my hand.

Penny raised an eyebrow. "I have good gossip. Remember your neighbor Dave?"

"Yes, why?"

Dave had lived in the cottage next to ours for most of his life. The last time I saw him had been the summer after I graduated from college. At the time, I thought he had been dating Elizabeth, but it didn't seem to stick. He was gone by the end of the summer, and Elizabeth never spoke about him again. His family had started renting their house to summer people. There were rumors about how they had a second and third mortgage and needed the rent to pay off the debt.

Penny gave me a wicked grin. "He's here and spending time with Elizabeth. Maybe they're back together?"

"Why is he back in town?"

She raised an eyebrow. "Someone at the bank told me his house is in foreclosure. Maybe he is looking for an heiress to marry?"

I almost choked on my own saliva. "I hope he knows Elizabeth is just as broke as she was when he dated her years ago. No, she has even less now. Unless you count wealth in shoes and purses."

"Only Elizabeth counts wealth that way," Penny said between giggles.

"Valid point."

"Basically, be careful. Your father hasn't been shy about telling people you have him on an allowance and are hoarding his money away for your own reasons. Elizabeth has been happy to confirm this and suggest you're keeping it for yourself."

"Oh, for fuck's sake!" I said, rubbing my temples.

"This is just a rumor, but consider yourself caught up."

I decided I needed to change the conversation. "Can you talk about your book?"

Penny shook her head. "Are you leaving your jackass publishing company?"

I frowned. "No."

"If you take that job in LA, I will be happy to sign a contract and let you see it. It is amazing. If you stay in your current shitshow, then I'm not handing it over."

"I'm going to use the Los Angeles job to improve my situation at work. I can't take it."

"Why the hell not? Ted has a point about Karen holding you back. I know she thinks she's helping you, but she isn't."

I thought about the reality I had been facing over the past month. "If there was a chance with Freddy, I would take it in a heartbeat."

"It's back to Freddy?"

"He will always be Freddy for me," I said in a low voice.

I could feel the tears fill up my eyes. Penny handed me the box of tissues she kept close at hand. She said nothing as I blew my nose and composed myself again.

"Don't make your decision around him. Maybe if he sees you around Los Angeles, he'll soften a bit. You remember your pro and con list you made before graduation after he proposed?"

"Yes, very much so."

"Write a new one for a move to LA," Penny said, handing me a pad of paper and a pencil.

Pro to move to LA:
- Fantastic job opportunity to be a partner in a publishing house and be in charge.
- Nice people who are potential friends.
- Other side of the country from my family and their co-dependence.

Cons to move to LA:
- I love him.

"The list is all reversed now," Penny said after I handed her the list.

I slumped back into the sofa we were sitting on. "Loving him wasn't enough last time, and it should have been."

"You're going to make the same choice, aren't you?"

I took the pad from her. "I don't know. If he wasn't so angry, it would all be different. Maybe I should use the job offer to change my situation here?"

Penny frowned. "That's not going to fix this, Emma. You have to make a big change. This is your car accident."

Chapter Twenty

My father dragged me to a beach concert that night. I agreed to avoid a fight. We sat on the beach alone in silence for a little while before Elizabeth found us. As Penny had warned, Dave seemed attached to Elizabeth at first. When he abandoned her to talk to me, I remembered more of what had happened that summer after leaving Chicago. Elizabeth had always been Dave's preferred sister when we were children because they were the same age. I was too bookish for his taste, and Mary was too needy. He seemed different when I came home after graduation.

Now I understand my behavior that summer better. I was trying to ignore the building depression by keeping busy because I couldn't be depressed if I was active and cheerful. I didn't act like myself because of this. I forced myself to be more outgoing and sociable than I naturally was. Elizabeth had once been bubbly and popular but always a mean girl. When I got back from college, she was mostly just mean. The more time Dave and I spent together, the meaner Elizabeth got. I wasn't in any frame of mind to want a new boyfriend. I didn't think, at the time, Dave was looking for more than someone nice to hang out with. Elizabeth had clearly felt otherwise.

I had never thought about Dave much during the following eight years, but here we all were again. I was trying to recover from my feelings about Fredrick while Dave and Elizabeth were flirting without any sense of commitment. I hoped Penny was wrong about him looking for someone with money. He was looking in the wrong direction if he was.

"It's been years since the last time we saw each other," Dave said as he sat down next to me on the blanket.

I closed the book I had been reading. It was something I had picked up at PubCon. "It has been about eight years. Are you back for good or just for part of the summer?" I asked.

"I'm trying to decide what to do about the house. My parents aren't going to come back. They've moved to Florida, so they don't need Cape Cod vacations."

I raised an eyebrow. "Are you tired of having a house you don't spend time in?"

Dave smiled. "Something like that. The rent isn't enough to cover the expenses. It would be smarter to sell."

We sat in silence for a moment.

"Elizabeth has been helping me catch up on all the things I missed. Things certainly have changed for all of you."

"Like what?" I asked.

"Oh, that she and your father moved to Westchester. She said you were just on a book tour. Was it fun?" he asked, trying to pull more information out of me.

I decided to give him some details. "I was doing a book tour for Fredrick Wentworth's new book."

He didn't look at me. "Oh, isn't it on the bestsellers list already?"

I smiled. "I'm good at my job."

Dave and I talked through most of the night. I ended up telling him some of the things that happened on the tour, including Louisa's accident. I tried to press him on his intentions with my sister, his financial situation, and other important issues, but he kept changing the subject to talk about me. I was equally evasive with some of his more personal questions. He had always been very pushy and invasive on personal issues. It felt like he was gathering information to use to his advantage.

"Are you going to the Musgroves' BBQ tomorrow?" Dave asked before we left the beach.

"It's a tradition. They are coming back from Chicago tonight."

"Louisa must be fine if they let her leave the city and come home."

"Knowing Louisa, it will be like nothing ever happened. If she wants something, the world tends to bend to her will."

I was right; Louisa had made a fast and complete recovery. I was happy to see Seth when I got to the house the next night. He had been invited to spend July with the Musgroves on Cape Cod.

"We're getting married!" Louisa said to me in private.

She pulled out a Tiffany blue ring box and showed off a huge, pretty diamond engagement ring.

My eyes got wide. "That was fast."

She put her finger over her lips. "Shhhh, he's officially proposing tonight. He said when I got hurt, he just knew he didn't want to live without me. It will take at least a year to plan the wedding, but I knew it when I met him. I knew I would marry him someday."

I tried to hide my smile. "I'm sure you let Fredrick down easily."

"Oh, silly, I was just flirting with him. He knows that," she said with a wink.

I totally missed the tense she used in that last sentence. If I had paid better attention, I wouldn't have been so surprised when I walked out to the deck and found Fredrick sitting there with Tommy drinking beer and monitoring the grill.

Chapter Twenty-One

I rushed back into the house and out the front door before Fredrick could see me. I sat on the front step and caught my breath before I pulled out my phone and began a text conversation with Penny.

Emma: FW is here - @ the Musgroves

Penny: Why

Emma: No clue - ran away B4 he saw me

Penny: Emma!

Emma: I can't do this again

Penny: You R a mature adult who can do 1 damn BBQ

Emma No I really don't think that's true

Penny: You had the fight, he apologized, move on

Emma: Or I could stay in the house and play with the boys

Penny: Or you could throw him on a bed and fuck his brains out.

I couldn't help chuckling at Penny's text.

Emma: Or I can go play with my nephews

Penny: I say sex!

Emma: Updates later - play with toddlers.

That's precisely what I did. I grabbed a beer, found my nephews, and played with them. Thing One (TJ) and Thing Two (Nathan) were born ten months apart. They had struggled to get pregnant the first time. My sister swore she knew she could get pregnant; she just thought the chances were unlikely.

"That's when the time is best for life to laugh at you," Karen had said when Mary got pregnant a month after Thing One was born.

I agreed, but I adore both boys so much that I never remind my sister that she's reckless. They're toddler boys with limited vocabulary and more energy than anyone knew what to do with. I got lucky and found them playing with their trucks when I got into the playroom. They were wearing their wet swimsuits, which were dripping into the carpet.

After twenty minutes, Seth came down to the playroom with Fredrick in tow. Neither child seemed very interested in the two men they didn't know. I was lying on my stomach making fire truck noises with Thing Two. My nephews both have their mother's need for constant praise and attention. Give one attention, and the other will want it, too. Years of dealing with their mother's attention needs had taught me to handle the boys, but Seth was trying to play with them and was out of his league.

"Emma, my turn!" Thing One yelled as he started to climb on my back.

"You can wait your turn," I said, trying to pull my nephew off.

"NO! Play with me," Thing One demanded as he grabbed my hair and pulled back.

Being wholly engrossed with fire trucks, Thing Two ignored his older brother. I kept trying to pull Thing One off my back, but he was out of reach, no matter which way I turned and moved. His wet clothes dripped on me and made me uncomfortable. He enjoyed the struggle, which turned it into a game of keep-away.

"Thomas, let go right now!" I demanded.

I hated having to resort to his given name. Next would be his full name.

"No!" Thing One said through his giggles.

When I felt him let go of me mid-giggle, I looked up to see Fredrick standing over me with Thing One in his arms.

"Let your aunt take a break. Let's go play on the beach!" Fredrick said, quickly turning away but not before I noticed his tight lips that almost looked like a snarl.

Both boys perked up at the idea of playing on the beach. Thing One jumped from Fredrick's arms and ran out of the room with Thing Two at his heels. Seth followed them while Fredrick helped me up. I felt a slight shiver run through my body as our hands met.

"Thank you," I whispered.

"My pleasure. They love you, but little boys have their own way of showing it," he said before walking out of the room, leaving me alone.

By the time I got back up to the patio, Seth, Fredrick, and the boys were gone. I found Dave standing off to the side, watching me.

"I heard you were here somewhere," Dave said and offered me a beer.

I shook my head and showed him the still-full bottle in my hand.

"I was just playing with the boys," I said before taking a sip.

"I just saw Louisa's boyfriend and Fredrick Wentworth run after two toddlers. My small brush with fame! They went down to the beach if you're looking for them."

I led Dave over to lounge chairs, where I collapsed. "The toddlers would be my nephews. They're exhausting."

Dave sat in the other. "Your sister seems to manage. Does that mean Auntie Elizabeth and Auntie Emma help out a lot?"

I let a small laugh escape my lips. "More like Auntie Emma, Auntie Louisa, and Nana. Elizabeth has no tolerance for children unless... no... no tolerance for children."

"Not even family?" Dave asked, raising an eyebrow.

"She just wasn't designed that way. Even worse, they sense her disdain, and she is the first one they go to with poopy diapers or messy hands. Many a designer bag and dress have been ruined."

"I don't remember Elizabeth like that," he said and squinted.

"There weren't any children around back then," Elizabeth said as she and my father walked outside.

My older sister was dressed immaculately. Her makeup was perfect, her hair was professionally done, and her clothes were perfectly pressed. She had been laughing at something my father said, the two of them in their own world.

Once the table was set and the food cooked, we all found our places at the dinner table on the deck. By the time Fredrick went to find a spot to sit, his only option was to sit next to Elizabeth. My older sister raised an eyebrow and looked Fredrick up and down before making the instantaneous decision that he was beneath her. With a flip of her hair, she turned in the other direction and spent the entire dinner talking to Dave and my father, who also sat close by. I was curious about their reactions to each other, and I got what I expected. I wasn't sure if I was amused or disappointed. My father had judged Fredrick the same way eight years ago. I knew what to expect, but part of me wished she had shown some interest in him, if only because he was famous.

Seth's proposal to Louisa happened in the middle of dinner. Everyone seemed excited for them, but I saw the smirk my father and Elizabeth exchanged. There was something snobby about it, and I was irritated by their reactions. Nobody was good enough for them. A famous actor and writer sat at a table with them, and both acted like it was an inconvenience. The longer we all spent at the table together, the angrier I got.

"Tomorrow, we're meeting again for the big fireworks production on the beach, right Walter?" Mr. Musgrove said while everyone was eating.

"Of course. Emma is going to the beach tomorrow to put the chairs and blankets out, so we get the best spot," my father said without even looking at me to confirm.

"No, I'm not doing that," I said without thinking.

Everyone stopped eating and looked at me. Even I was surprised by what I had said; it felt good to say it.

"Excuse me?" my father said, finally meeting my eyes.

I decided to embrace my act of defiance. I sat back in the chair and crossed my arms. "If you want the spot on the beach that will assure you are seen by a Kennedy, then do it yourself. I'm not your slave."

"You always do it," Elizabeth whined.

"You're both adults. One of you is actually a parent, and neither has a job. I have work to do," I said and added a shrug.

"But Emma, you're on vacation," Mary said.

"I am tired of playing servant," I said, not sure where this boldness was coming from but feeling great as I let out all my frustrations. "I'm going to sit where I want, with the people I want, and I might not even go anyway. Plus, I am tired of being the adult in this family. Nobody ever does anything for me or asks me what I want. Everyone just assumes I will take care of Walter and Elizabeth for the rest of their lives. You would think you're disabled, the way you expect me to do things for you. I actually have a friend who is disabled, and she does more for herself than either of you have ever done. Oh, boo-hoo, you're sad because Mom died. You know what? I miss her too! I am sad she died too, but do you see me falling apart and not getting on with my life. It's been nearly fifteen years. She would be disgusted by the two of you. Mary, she would probably be proud of, but the three of us would disgust her. I'm done. I'm going to think of me and only me for the first time in years. Sorry, not sorry!"

I finally stopped to take a breath and realized I was on my feet. I could feel my pulse racing, and my face was hot. Everyone spoke at once. There was indignation that I would even consider not going to a family tradition. There was anger that I accused my father of treating his daughter as an indentured servant. My father insisted this was inappropriate behavior and that I was acting like a spoiled child throwing a temper tantrum. Mary demanded I was needed to take care of the boys. Louisa begged me to reconsider and not ruin such a wonderful week. Elizabeth was close to having a tantrum of her own. The only one who didn't say anything was Fredrick, who silently looked at me, an eyebrow raised as he fought a smile.

I stormed off without another word.

"Emma, wait!" I heard Fredrick call from behind me after I had left the house and started to walk home.

I stopped and let him catch up to me.

"You shouldn't walk home alone at night. You could get hit by a car, or who knows what else. Let me walk with you," he said, his arms stiff by his side.

My pulse was still racing, and I fought the desire to stomp away. "What the fuck do you care for? It's not like I mean anything to you anymore."

He took a step away from me. "That's not fair. I would feel much better if you let me walk with you because I think you're drunk. You certainly aren't walking in a straight line."

"Whatever," I said, but he was right, and my earlier meltdown made more sense.

We walked alone in silence for a while. Every so often, he would take my arm to steady me. I couldn't figure out how I had gotten drunk on one beer that I had nursed all night.

"It was a last-minute decision to come out here with the Musgroves," Fredrick suddenly said. "When they learned I had never been to Cape Cod, they wouldn't take no for an answer. I should have spoken to you about it first. I'm sorry I just showed up."

I was focused on walking. "They'll make sure you enjoy yourself."

"Don't you like it out here?"

I knew I shouldn't have kept talking, but that didn't stop me. "I love it out here. I just happen to not like my family much at the moment."

"Was it this bad when we were at college?" Fredrick asked in a low voice.

I remembered what it was like before I went to college, but I rarely came home for long periods during the four years in Chicago. It was easy to forget what was happening to my family in New York when you weren't with them.

I briefly shook my head, only stopping because the world began to spin. "I don't remember it being this bad before I left, but I was grieving my mother's death. When I got home, it was like this."

Fredrick was quiet for a moment. I don't know if I had ever let him into my grief. "Dealing with them is why you're always prepared for a crisis, isn't it?"

I let out a deep sigh. "Probably."

I felt his hand slip into mine and squeeze. "You were amazing in Chicago. I really am sorry I was so nasty to you. Louisa pretty much worships you now that you saved her life."

Fredrick pulled me to the side of the road. We saw car lights come up from behind us. When the car stopped next to us, Dave lowered the window on the driver's side.

"I thought you could use a ride," Dave said with a look that suggested he was very impressed with himself.

I could see a snarl pass over Fredrick's face.

"You should take it. You're probably safer in a car," Fredrick said, leading me to the passenger side door and opening it.

For a moment, I considered refusing the ride to walk with Fredrick but decided it was safer this way. "Thank you, Fredrick," I said as he closed the door.

"Emma, come to the fireworks tomorrow night. Promise me you won't punish yourself because you're tired of your family's behavior," Fredrick said as I rolled down the window to let in the cool night air.

Chapter Twenty-Two

Thing One and Thing Two had been upset after dinner and insisted on sleeping with me. They were all assuming I was happy to take responsibility for my sister's children. When my father brought them back to the house, I took charge but never got a simple thank you from anyone. Nothing seemed to change as a result of my outburst.

I came down for breakfast the following day to find my father sitting with Karen. When he saw me, he got up and left the room. Karen gave me a quick hug.

"I understand you stood up for yourself last night. I am very impressed," Karen said.

I didn't want to talk about it yet. I made myself tea and oatmeal and told Karen about the tour. I didn't mention that Fredrick was here on the Cape. I had other things to bring up before sharing that.

"Your father said Louisa is engaged. I didn't realize she was even dating anyone," Karen said as she poured herself a second cup of coffee. There was a broken muffin on the plate at her spot. I was positive she hadn't eaten any.

"She met Seth on the book tour in Los Angeles," I said as I sat down and pulled a muffin from the platter sitting on the table.

I wondered who had pulled out the muffins and arranged them nicely on a platter for each of us to eat as we wanted. I was sure Karen knew neither my father nor Elizabeth would think to accommodate a guest.

Karen looked at me as she continued to pick apart the mangled muffin in front of her. "So, she had a good tour, and you had a bad one."

"I don't know if I would call it a bad one. It wasn't how I would have chosen to spend my time, but it did give me a chance to think about what is going on," I said, hoping I sounded nonchalant.

Karen gave me a tight smile. "What do you mean about what's going on?"

I looked her in the eye. "Fredrick's agent sent me his manuscript, but I never saw it. How is that possible?"

Karen's mouth fell open, and she got pale but didn't say a word.

"I don't want to assume anything because that's not fair, but I was told that you passed the manuscript on to Christi, who saw a draft full of my notes from eight years ago," I continued when she didn't respond.

"You didn't need him in your life again. You've moved on," Karen said in a whisper.

I took a sip of my tea to give me time to carefully consider my response. "This isn't about Fredrick right now. This is about how I am treated professionally. Right now, I understand that you have been watching my emails and interceding when you don't like something. I can't help but wonder, considering how agents wanted a contractual commitment to working with me, how many people have been passed on before I knew they existed."

Karen opened her mouth to respond, and I put a hand up, not wanting to let her interrupt me. "You are clearly in a difficult situation because of your own choices, but I'm increasingly confident that our bosses now consider me a problem. This is why I was forced to go on a book tour with one of those authors. Is my future with this company at risk?"

Karen looked down and pursed her lips before whispering. "You work for me, not them."

"If that were true," I said, "you would have been able to keep me from spending the last month babysitting Fredrick. To be honest, I was the only reason he needed babysitting. Our history made us both miserable, and it could have derailed the tour. It would have made things worse."

Karen opened her mouth to speak again, but her face was red, and I was confident that she would defend herself. I wasn't in the mood to hear excuses. Her response had confirmed my theories, and now I had to decide one last thing. There was nobody around me who could advise me about this decision. It was on my shoulders.

Later that day, Karen and I packed some dinner and walked down to the beach with Thing One and Thing Two in tow. As soon as they saw Mary, they ran to her demanding food and attention. Fortunately, she was ready to supply both. Fredrick was sitting next to Seth and Louisa. I know Karen saw him, but she ignored him. There was still plenty of tension between us after our conversation that morning. She prattled on about how lucky we were to get such good spots. Fredrick looked back at me and smiled.

"Is this a good spot to get the attention of a Kennedy?" I heard Dave ask from behind me.

"Who the hell knows," I said with a shrug. "Do you remember anyone from the family coming here?"

Dave chuckled and shook his head. "Your father swears someone with the last name Kennedy is coming tonight."

I leaned closer to him and whispered. "Honestly, if Eddie and Little Eddie Bouvier Beale showed up, he would consider that a Kennedy showing up."

"Those are the hoarders from the Hamptons, right?" Dave asked with a smirk.

"Yes! The ones who got a movie out of it. My father can hoard like a champ, so I think they would get along wonderfully."

The two of us laughed for a moment. "Wait, isn't one dead?" Dave asked.

"Both are dead," I said as I tried to stop laughing.

I walked over to the cooler to find something cold to drink. I only found beer.

"There's water on the bottom," Fredrick said as he walked over.

I dug to the bottom, letting the ice water cool me off. "Good, beer now would mean I would be drunk in a heartbeat. It's much too hot," I said and pulled out a cold bottle of water.

I looked up to see my father acting like a social butterfly wandering from group to group, saying hello to old friends.

"Your father seems to be happy," Fredrick said, nodding his head in my father's direction.

My face fell. "He's with his social equals and betters. He's in hog heaven."

"You're very hard on him. I get it with Elizabeth, but your dad... he clearly hasn't gotten over your mother's death. Losing the person you love the most in the world can do odd things to people," Fredrick said, and our eyes locked.

"I lost her too, and I manage to act like an adult," I said without breaking eye contact.

Fredrick sighed and looked away before I walked back to my beach chair, sat down, opened a book, and waited for it to get dark.

My father insisted someone related to the Kennedys did show up that night. I never saw anyone aside from the people who had been coming to the beach on the Fourth of July for years.

I spent most of the day deciding what to do about work, and I needed to talk to someone about it. Before the fireworks started, I had the sudden urge to sit next to Fredrick and talk. I had already drunk a few beers, and I was a bit intoxicated, but at the time, asking his advice felt like the best idea ever. Thinking back, I am shocked my first instinct wasn't to tackle him and make out with him.

I came close to doing it, and I moved my chair, but Dave followed me. When I tried to talk to Fredrick, Dave interrupted and started asking questions about my job and asking weird questions about hiding money. I was confused and annoyed with him. I had made the mistake of being too friendly and open with him. I felt like we were repeating that summer eight years ago after leaving Chicago. He seemed to have abandoned Elizabeth in favor of me, but I wasn't encouraging it this time. I wanted him to leave me alone.

Fredrick left the fireworks early, offering to help Tommy take the boys home when Thing Two had a meltdown that triggered Thing One to join his younger brother. When the show was over, I felt like an idiot. I had momentarily forgotten that Fredrick no longer loved me and wanted me. I had lost his good opinion of me a long time ago, and he had made it clear. Just because he was nicer to me didn't mean he wanted me around. I felt like a drunk and desperate fool. I was acting toward Fredrick the same way Dave was acting toward me.

"Tomorrow, you need to take me to the craft store," Louisa said as we packed up our stuff.

"Why?"

Louisa looked around and lowered her voice. "I need to look at wedding stuff. I need to decide what to make myself and what to buy. I have been on Pinterest, Emma. There are so many cute ideas!" She squealed the last sentence, and I wondered why she bothered lowering her voice.

"Louisa, you're the least crafty person I know," I said.

"Exactly! If there's something I need to make, I need time to perfect it. Please, please, please, Emma! We can go to the fancy yarn shop and maybe also look at dresses, and I'll buy you lunch. I promise something good for lunch too!"

I smiled, excited she wanted me to be involved. "Ok, you're driving then."

Louise bounced in place and rapidly clapped her hands. "Great! I'll pick you up at eleven!"

Chapter Twenty-Three

Mary was with Louisa when she arrived. I expected her to tag along. Mary would not want to be left out of any trip that included wedding planning. I pretended to be a bit hungover and wandered around the big craft shop. Louisa and Mary went directly to the wedding section while I made my way back to the inexpensive yarn. My coping mechanism has always been yarn. I had the sudden desire to knit blankets and was picking out the yarn when I got a text message from Penny.

Penny: Are you going to marry Dave?

Emma: What? No!

Penny: Oh, thank god. I was worried you had lost your head.

Emma: Why would you think that?

Penny: The woman who preps my meals just came in and told me the whole town is talking.

Emma: About what?

Penny: You and Dave - that you're in love?

Emma: Where the hell did that come from?

Penny: You were seen on the beach last night.

Emma: FFS FW was right there too!

Penny: Would Elizabeth spread that rumor?

Emma: Only if she thought she had something to gain.

Penny: I thought she wanted him?

Emma: Dave? She hasn't been paying attention to him.

Penny: Emma - what if he's spreading it? Maybe he's dangerous!

"Penny thinks who is dangerous, Emma?"

I looked up to see Tommy reading over my shoulder, and he looked concerned. Seth and Fredrick were standing close by.

"Nobody, it's nothing," I said in practically one word.

"We were wondering where you disappeared to. We actually argued. Mary insisted you were in the kid's section, and I thought maybe the baskets. Fredrick actually suggested we look in the yarn section. After a month together, he clearly discovered your weakness," Tommy said with a grin.

I wondered if Fredrick had told Tommy about our history.

"It really wasn't that difficult to guess. She always had knitting with her on tour, even if she never touched it," Fredrick said with a shrug.

"Come on; we're hungry. We're a table for six at lunch, and Seth is treating. He's going to learn what it means to be part of this family," Tommy said, leading the group away.

Tommy wandered around the store just like his sons. He was easily distracted by something and needed to touch it. Seth and I walked together, moving slowly towards the front of the store. Fredrick brought up the rear, typing on his cellphone. I assumed he was text messaging someone important.

"Don't let Tommy intimidate you," I said to Seth.

Seth silently laughed. "He's trying to force years of intimidation into a few weeks. I can take it. I only care about what Louisa wants."

"What does she want?" I asked.

He raised an eyebrow. "We're debating whether to move to LA or New York. We're both happy to live in either city. We just can't decide."

I smiled, happy that they were talking about this in a way Fredrick and I had never been able to. "I thought she was going to take over for me with book tours? She's willing to give that up?"

"We are actually talking about living on both coasts. She wants to try spending most of the year in LA and then summer out here. That way, she can see her family but not be around them all the time. She thinks her parents drive Mary and Tommy crazy."

"Mary may pretend they drive her crazy, but she really loves the attention."

"I figured that," Seth said, tilting his head to the side. "Your other sister, Elizabeth, she is a real piece of work."

"You can say it, Seth. Elizabeth is a bitch."

***

171

I felt uncomfortable during lunch. I felt out of sync with Fredrick there, watching me around my family and friends. It had been easier on the book tour when we had both been out of our element or back in New York, where our lives overlapped for moments. With him as a guest of the Musgroves, I felt like there was no escaping him. He would see a version of me that he had never been exposed to in our relationship. As a result, I shut down, getting quieter as lunch went on.

It seemed to go unnoticed around me. While Seth and Louisa only had eyes for each other, Mary and Tommy had a fight about their evening plans. My father had decided to host a dinner party. I wasn't sure how he would manage that and who was going to cook, but the invitations had gone out in a flurry of text messages. Mary wanted to go to the dinner in case someone important came. Tommy wanted a date night away from the family. He had arranged to take the family boat out for a romantic dinner and (although not said) sex. Fredrick and I both spent lunch looking at our cell phones. I was playing Scrabble. I tried not to pay attention to him, but he seemed to be sending text messages to someone. I wondered if the other person was Patrick or a woman who had been unmentioned so far. There was no reason to think that, but the more I did, the more irritated I got. Fredrick was mine. We were supposed to be together.

"Emma," Tommy said, pulling me into the argument. "What would you rather do? Go to your father's dinner or go out on the water in a boat and have a romantic dinner?"

I blinked a few times to process the question and decide the best answer. "Who is going to be at dinner?" I asked, trying to buy myself time.

"Everyone!" Mary said, raising an eyebrow. "Even Dave will be there."

Everyone was looking at me, even Fredrick. I was irritated that people kept thinking I wanted Dave. Yet again, Penny knew the good gossip before I did. I opened my mouth to answer but glanced at Fredrick, who looked at the table and shook slightly. He was afraid of what I might say. I thought about everything Fredrick might have seen in the past few days and Mary's penchant for talking without thinking. Did I still have a chance with Fredrick?

I took a deep breath, ready to take a chance. "I would rather have an evening on the boat than spend another evening with Dave. Wait, let me clarify. I would rather spend an evening on a bed of broken glass than spend another night with Dave."

Louisa and Seth both laughed. I hoped that would shut down any family's expectations or any fear Fredrick had about my future with Dave.

"Would you rather re-do the entire book tour than spend another night with Dave?" Louisa asked, narrowing her eyes and pointing at me.

I turned and looked at Fredrick; he looked directly into my eyes.

"Anything would be better than another night with Dave."

***

I had to spend another night with Dave. I also spent another night with Fredrick, so... it wasn't the worst night.

The party wasn't what my father had hoped but, as Karen reminded him, many people already had plans for the evening. Mary and Tommy went for their romantic boat ride, but Louisa and Seth brought Fredrick. Seth was a very good sport and spent the evening talking with me to help keep Dave away. Fredrick seemed to hover nearby off and on. He was glued to his cellphone, texting away like crazy. I must have been wrong about having a chance with him. If he had wanted another chance, I had made sure the door was firmly open. I wanted to hurt whoever was on the other side of those text messages.

"Your parents look very much in love," Seth said, looking at some of the family photos my father kept on display. "What was her name?"

The two of us were sitting in the den with tea and dessert. I looked at the picture of my parents placed between our chairs. "Her name was Violet, and they were," I said and remembered once dreaming of having that partner in my life.

Seth lowered his voice as he leaned on the arm of his chair. "The Musgroves think he'll never get over her death."

I could feel the tears start to fill my eyes, and I wiped them away. "I think he could if he wanted to. Had it been reversed and he had died, my mother would have fallen apart, too."

"Was she that dependent on him?"

I nodded. "Financially, he was the breadwinner. She put her career on hold to raise the three of us. She was just trying to get back to editing when she got sick. It had not been going well for her, from what I remember. I think it would have been worse for her to be both emotionally and financially destroyed. In my experience, women suffer more when a relationship ends. Men just seem to move on."

Seth raised an eyebrow. "I think you're wrong. Obviously, your father hasn't just moved on."

"I think he's the exception, not the rule."

Seth shook his head. "I know popular culture likes to think that only a woman grieves the end of a relationship, but men have been taught to not let others see them grieve. Women have the freedom to mourn and move on to the next relationship. Men never get that chance to learn how to grieve. Instead, we keep it inside and are taught emotions are bad."

I turned in my seat to give Seth my full attention. My sadness about my mother dissipated as I thought about how my relationship with Fredrick ended and was mourned. "That's not fair. Women may know how to emote better, but we hold on to each broken heart. When we have loved someone, we compare every person to them. How many women stay in bad relationships because they're in love? Even if there is no chance in the world for a reunion with the one she loves, a woman will always live in a state of hope that it could happen and agony that it hasn't. Maybe we can pretend we are ok, but deep down, we really aren't. Sometimes, we think we've moved on, but we really regret our decision. We have to live with that regret."

"Men don't really move on either, Emma. They pretend they're fine and try to forget, too. That may be why it seems men move on quickly. It's a way for them to avoid their emotions. For example, some men find women completely different from the one they loved. I imagine some women do the same. An example, in that case, is a woman who takes the reasons she left a relationship and overachieves at making sure they are accurate."

Before I could respond, there was the clatter of a cell phone falling on the floor. I looked over to see Fredrick sitting close by and realized he had heard the entire conversation. Seth didn't even glance over at Fredrick. Clearly, Seth had known Fredrick had been sitting right there.

"So, what about you, Emma? Did you embrace your emotions so you could move on, or did you avoid them?" Seth asked, tilting his head to the side.

"I think I did a little bit of both. Now I live in a state of hope and agony - constantly," I said with a smile and got up.

I left the house and hid outside until I heard cars leaving. I spent the time thinking about what Seth had said. No, I hadn't embraced my emotions at all. I had put them in a box so I could move on. On the other hand, Fredrick had aired his grief for the world to see. I wasn't allowing the world to happen to me because I hadn't embraced my feelings. Even now, avoiding a decision about my career was another way of avoiding my feelings for Fredrick. I wanted the job Ted was offering me. Even if it meant I had to see Fredrick every day, I wanted to be in control of my life again.

Before I went to bed that night, I sent an email to Ted and told him I would take the job and suggested some times to talk about the details.

Chapter Twenty-Four

I woke up the next morning to the tweeting of my cell phone.

Fred: Did you get my email?

Emma: Email? Hold on- let me check

I checked my personal email, and there was nothing there from Fredrick.

Emma: Nope. Nothing. When did you send it?

Fred: Two days ago. Think it got lost?

Emma: What email address do you have for me?

It was my work email. There was nothing in my inbox, but then I remembered what Karen had done with his past email. I checked the spam server. This was a system each of us could set up to make sure the spam never got to us. Each of us could set rules to direct the server. I wasn't surprised when I found a folder with a bunch of emails from Fredrick and his agent. I looked at the details and saw Karen had set it up, and notifications were sent to her. I quickly found an email from two days ago with the subject: Give it a quick edit? I didn't waste time and released all the emails to my account but not before taking a screenshot of the page just in case.

The email was a link to a Google Doc named: *Emma*.

I set my phone to not disturb me and pulled out my iPad so I could easily make the edits or, at the very least, read it better. I sat down in the chair in my bedroom and read Fredrick Wentworth's new novel.

Emma

I knew I would see her in New York. I had been told she would be there. Everyone working on my book talked about her like a publishing goddess. She knew how to organize amazing book tours. She was the Queen of Book Tours. She could pick award winners and best sellers after reading a few pages. If she had edited Twilight, it would have been a good book or not been published. She hadn't even bothered to respond when my agent sent her this book, but she had to know I would be there too.

She left me to have this. I had always thought she had made the wrong decision, but listening to Christi and her team made me reconsider. Maybe she had made the right choice? I wondered if she ever thought of me. There wasn't a day that went by that she wasn't in my thoughts. Every single woman I dated after Emma was an attempt to forget her. My friends, none of whom had ever and would ever meet her, think she's the devil. To be fair, when I wrote a movie about how I tried to get over our breakup, I lied a lot. Not just about her, but about the fact that I got over it. I demonized her so I could forget her. It never worked.

Patrick had been with me every step of the way from the moment I had sent the book to an agent. Now I would be away for a month promoting this book, and he would join me after the publishing convention. This book was older than anything else I had written. Christi knew someone else had edited it. She had seen the draft Emma had given me with her edits, which I had never made. I didn't have the will to tell her that her favorite colleague actually edited it already. I wasn't surprised when she came back with only a few changes. Patrick assured me New York would be fantastic.

"New York is Emma," I said to Patrick.

Patrick sat on my bed with a sigh.

"If you need me to come early, I can. I don't have to wait until the actual tour starts."

"I'm going to see her. I know it. She will be at this conference. She will be the belle of the ball."

"You are being an idiot."

"She probably told everyone about her evil ex-Fredrick who wanted to pull her away from her dreams and force her to live in hot and vapid Los Angeles. They all probably know the movie was about her. They are all probably pretending to be nice to me."

"You changed her name. I am sure nobody knows," Patrick said, waving his hand to dismiss my concerns. "Don't you think they would have refused to publish the book if she had told everyone all these things?"

He was right.

I saw her almost as soon as I arrived. I knew her from behind. Her long brown hair pulled back in a clip. The way she sat in the chair talking to one of the most famous writers in the world. The way she laughed. I love the way she laughs. She throws her head back, and it's a mix of a belly laugh with a little tinkling laugh. Hearing it was like a punch in the gut. Hearing it put me back to where I was when I met her ten years before. The moment I saw her was when I decided I wanted to spend the rest of my life looking into her eyes, kissing her lips, and touching her face. I wanted her to smile at me that way forever, and she hadn't even met me yet. There was a huskiness to her voice that sent shivers down my spine. I had never reacted this way to a woman.

I was jello every time I was in a room with her. I couldn't talk to her until I had something specific to say. Once I started talking, there was no limit to what we could talk about. The more I learned about her, the more positive I was that she was the only woman I would ever love.

She made the first move, but we were drunk, and I couldn't do what I wanted. She insisted I sleep in her bed that night even if I wasn't going to have awkward first-time sex with her. She smiled as she fell asleep. I lay in her bed, which smelled like cherry blossoms, and never wanted to get up. I promised myself if she still wanted me in the morning, I would never deny her anything ever again. I woke up as soon as I felt her lips and breath on my neck. She was still asleep. She had rolled into my body. She had wrapped her arms around me and pressed her body to mine. I closed my eyes and thought of dead puppies and baseball, not opening my eyes until she woke up. There she was, looking right into my eyes with her bright green ones. I remember the sex being awkward. It was only awkward that once. Once I knew her body and made a point of learning it quickly, I knew exactly what to do.

I shouldn't have proposed at graduation. I knew what she wanted from life. I knew her goals could really only be achieved in New York. I didn't care. I thought I could make her happy, and she would find new goals if she gave up everything she had ever wanted. When she refused to answer, I thought it was because she wanted me to propose in front of her father. I never got a chance to do that. As soon as Walter Shaw met me, he had no use for me. I was beneath him, and he clearly did not want his beloved daughter with me. Her mentor and mother's best friend, Karen, accompanied Walter to graduation. Neither of her sisters came. She didn't seem to mind either. In fact, I think she was annoyed that her father had come. She shut me out soon after they arrived. I realized when my parents insisted they join us for a joint graduation dinner that she would refuse me.

I felt like an idiot. I had ignored everything she had ever told me. I hadn't even considered other ways to be with her in two different cities or going to New York with her. By the time I realized I could have lived in New York, at least until a better solution had presented itself, she was gone. I spent my first summer at home in my childhood bedroom, depressed, high, and hungry. I don't know why I wrote the movie, but it was the only way to cope with everything. When I watched the completed movie for the first time, a few years later, I realized I had been cruel and childish. I regretted it, but there was no way to take it back now. I waited for a lawsuit, but nothing ever came.

Now she was there and so close. I decided to change my entire prepared speech. When Louisa introduced us, as if we had no idea the other ever existed in the world, Emma just looked at me. She had changed and looked worn out and faded. Her green eyes had lost their playful sparkle. I was angry at her for becoming a shell of herself. If she had stayed with me, this never would have happened. She showed no emotion as I spoke to a room of people about how important she had been to this book I had written. I didn't mention her name, but she had to know. She waited until her friend Tom spoke and then left right away. I asked him about it.

"The book is about her mother," Tom told me when the panel was over.

"Really?"

"The family has never gotten over her death," he said, giving me a copy of the book.

I scanned the pages quickly. I had never considered the impact of her mother's death on Emma. Life in Chicago must have been a way to escape her grief. She never wanted to talk about it beyond the basics. Her father's arrival at graduation would have been like a shock to the system after years away from it. I wanted to run up to the convention floor, find her, and wrap her in my arms. I wanted to make her better, but there wasn't time. I had to do a book signing.

She was everywhere. Every time I looked up, I saw her face. Every time I walked into a room, she was there. Sometimes she didn't even see me, but I always saw her. Sometimes she was alone, but occasionally she was with that woman who had convinced her to give up our life together. Seeing Karen with Emma brought back the anger I had felt eight years ago. Emma was still under her influence, and I let my anger flare where everyone could see it. I forgot that anger again when Emma sat across from me at my signing. For a while, she just stared blankly into space. Eventually, she looked at me and smiled. It was my smile, the smile that made everything ok and made me feel like there was nobody else in her world but me.

I got back to my hotel that night and dreamt of that smile.

My book was the source of all the trouble that followed. They underestimated the demand from the public attendees on the last day. Louisa, who had been there when the attack happened, found me at my hotel right away. She said the people who came that day were not part of the publishing industry. They were just people who had been allowed to buy tickets.

"Like Comic-Con?" I asked her when she came to my hotel after it happened.

Louisa was like many women I had dated since breaking up with Emma. It was clear, although she seemed to know Emma well, Louisa didn't know about our relationship.

Louisa put her hand on my arm. "Totally like it. Except nobody seems to have understood what that's like."

"The security at a Comic-Con is intense. You have to pay for items at a comic con, even an autograph."

"Right, so they told people they would get free books. Christi was worried that we didn't have enough, but we had no idea how many people to expect. We thought they would be grateful for what they had been able to get. One man just wouldn't take no and attacked her."

I hadn't been there when it happened. I was mystified by the intensity of the situation. These people weren't even getting my autograph or a picture.

"So, the tour is canceled?" I asked.

"Oh! No, no, no! Don't worry. The Queen of Book Tours is taking over."

"Emma?"

"Yep, she is going to take Christi's place, and she's amazing."

I had dinner with Christi, Louisa, Emma, and their family the night before the accident. It was uncomfortable, but I finally got to meet Mary. Mary may look like Emma, but they are nothing alike. Emma sat there in silence, looking irritated and a bit drunk. I waited for Emma to do something rash like she typically did when drunk. I didn't really know what to say, nor did I have a chance to say anything. Mary talked all night. Even Tommy, her husband, kept his mouth shut, but he was probably used to this. Nobody got a word in unless they asked a direct question. I wondered if Emma even liked her sister. I was surprised when, as we were leaving, I heard Emma tell Louisa not to call me Freddy. Emma knows that she is the only person who has ever been allowed to call me Freddy.

I sat in my hotel room bathroom and drank for about thirty minutes before calling Patrick and telling him everything.

"I'm about to get on the plane. I'll be there for dinner," Patrick said without hesitation.

The original plan was for him to meet me in Boston, the first tour stop outside of New York City. Now that I knew Emma was taking Christi's place, I was relieved Patrick would be there. More than anyone of my friends, he knew how heartbroken I had been when I returned from Chicago. He would help me stay focused now that I spent a week with the woman who had broken my heart.

"While I am very excited to finally meet the she-beast who destroyed you," Patrick said as soon as he found me at the airport, "I'm going to keep the two of you apart as much as I can. I will stay with you through LA like we planned. I emailed Christi during the flight. She thinks she can be mobile by the time you get back to New York at the end of the month. I will evaluate the situation when we get to LA and decide if I need to stay. Hopefully, she won't want to make trouble, and we can focus on just getting your book sold."

"Can you just do all the talking? I really don't know what I will say if I have to talk to her."

"Just talk to her when you have to talk. Keep it simple. I'll be your go-between."

Louisa, Mary, and Tommy were back to pick us up for dinner. Apparently, while drunk at dinner the night before, I
had agreed to have dinner with them again. We ate quickly
on 10th Ave, and the dinner was less stressful without
Emma there. It was a good thing that Tommy was good
company.

"We have to show you Columbus Circle and get dessert!"
Mary said.

"You have a book signing there tomorrow!" Louisa said.

"We must get Emma first," Mary said with a wink.

I had a momentary thought Mary was trying to set me
up with her sister. That was how I ended up standing
in Emma's small apartment. It wasn't what I expected,
but I should have. The apartment was about five hundred square feet, and the six of us made it feel crowded.
It was modern and full of books. There were a few family
pictures, including one of her mother, that I had looked
at often when it sat in our bedroom. It always amazed
me how much Emma looks like her mother. Even looking
at Mary, I can see their mother in both of them. Part of
me wanted to meet her older sister, Elizabeth, to see if
she too resembled their mother. There was no evidence
of another person in the apartment. Emma seemed to live
alone surrounded by her books and family - the reasons she
had insisted she couldn't say yes to marrying me.

I wanted to touch her, even just her hair. There was some
weird shift that night. I saw a side of Emma I had never

seen before: overly accommodating. At first, I assumed it was to avoid me when she agreed to sit with Mary while the rest of us went for ice cream. I couldn't help letting my very intimate knowledge of Emma guide me through the night. She seemed to appreciate my decision to get her something decent to eat since we had pulled her away from whatever dinner plans she had. Maybe it was a date with someone. Maybe it was just eating alone. I didn't want to know, but I was obsessed with imagining the possibilities. When we got back, I realized she genuinely liked Mary. I saw her smile at her sister and laugh with her.

"I'm in love," Patrick said in the hotel bar later that night.

"Tommy is straight, and you're both married," I said before taking a long drink of my beer.

"Tommy is nothing. I love Emma. I'm sorry, I'm the worst friend on the planet, but I am. I am! I love her. If she had rejected me, I would have been worse than you were. I understand everything now. She has already broken my heart by being a straight woman. I'm going to adopt her like a puppy."

"Please, don't do anything," I said as I motioned for the bartender to bring me another drink.

"Victor is going to flip over her. Sammy is going to love her," Patrick continued in his stream-of-consciousness monologue. "She's nothing like I expected. Louisa is what I expected from Emma. Louisa is like all those little pixie, blond girls you seem to like. Emma, she is a goddess... a tall, brunette, green-eyed goddess. That jaw, those shoulders, those BOOTS! This is true love, Fredrick.

Also, if Louisa calls you Freddy one more time, I am going to smack her."

"Please don't do that either."

Patrick sighed and drank his vodka tonic. It calmed him down, and he was able to focus again. "Emma has agreed to minimal contact. I'm going to say this now, and I want you to hear me. Are you ready?"

"Sure," I said with a shrug.

"She is still in love with you."

I scoffed. "No, she isn't at all."

"I bet you a hundred bucks that before this tour is over, she will be in your bed and naked."

"You've clearly lost your mind."

"Take the bet then."

"You're on. There is no way she would even consider letting me touch her, let alone get her naked and into my bed."

It was Patrick's turn to scoff. "I say we start by getting her drunk! I recall that worked very well the first time."

I barely remember the details of the book tour when Emma wasn't there. It was like someone kept flicking a light off and on. Every time she walked into a room, I had to fight the urge to kiss her and hold her. I tried to focus on my job: read, respond to questions, sign autographs. I listened to her chant her little cuppa tea song each time she brought me tea. She remembered exactly what I liked and the way I liked it. She would sit in the crowd with

Patrick and smile at me as if I was the center of the world. She would sit at dinners and go over the next day's plan with Patrick. Then she would be gone, and the light would go off again. She filled my fantasies at night as I dreamt of her. I woke up, sure I was feeling her lips on mine. I would roll over in bed, expecting to find her there. My morning fantasy was that she would be sprawled far away from me on the other side of these massive king-sized beds, but the tips of her fingers would be touching mine. It had been years since I had felt this way or thought of her this much, and it was torture.

My worlds collided the night of the benefit: Emma and Abby. Abby, like Emma, had wanted a life in New York. She hated LA and couldn't get away fast enough. I had sworn to myself that I would never live in New York as long as there was Emma in the world. I couldn't live in the same city as Emma knowing there was a chance I would run into her. The possibility of seeing her with another man, with her own family, or happy without me was too much. The reason Abby and I broke up was the reason I broke up with every other woman in the past eight years. None of them was the one woman I wanted.

By the time Abby arrived at the benefit, I was already immersed in Emma. She had touched me, fixed my tie, and called me Freddy. Her voice was the only one that made that nickname sound right. All I could smell were the cherry blossoms of her perfume. I could still feel where she had touched my face.

"This is my world," she said to me.

She was right. Our worlds were different. In hers, she went to library benefits, publishing conferences and ate out at classy restaurants all the time. In my world, I drank beer, sat naked in my house playing video games, got high with friends, ate junk food, and wrote. How could I have ever imagined we would end up together?

"I need to talk to you," Abby said to me when I got her away from Patrick and Emma.

"I'm sorry Patrick is being nasty. He thinks he is protecting me. What is it that you need to say?"

Abby kept looking back at Emma. "I'm sorry about how this is playing out in the press. The timing was a disaster, but I need to make sure you're ok. You don't have a good track record with rejection."

I took a deep breath and shut my eyes for a moment. "You need to back off. You made your decision, and I respect that. I have to deal with this my way."

Abby gestured toward the room. "You're at a party with Emma. I thought you hated her?"

"One, I'm here on a book tour, and, two, she is here professionally."

"You let her publish your book?"

"It's none of your business, but no. There was an emergency, and she was asked to take over."

I couldn't tell her the truth; that Emma had rejected my book like she had rejected me. At least she passed it on to someone else in the company.

Abby looked into my eyes. "She's not what I expected."

Abby may not look like Emma, but I had repeated the mistakes. Both had been clear about what they wanted, but I never walked away. I felt I could change their minds, but I was wrong. At least I wasn't really that in love with Abby.

I was never sure what to make of Louisa. I decided, after Los Angeles, that she's one of those women who flirts with everyone. It kept me sane. While Patrick entertained Emma, Louisa entertained me. Did she ever want more than a flirtation? I don't know, but as soon as we got to LA and met Seth, she was clear she was done with me. The LA stop of the tour was more intense than every other city. Emma showed up at every party. My friends adored her. Some even tried to seduce her. I was drunk and high at every party. That didn't shut out anything I was feeling. It amplified it. All these parties were for me, and I acted like an asshole. Sammy told me so after the first party. Once Patrick put Emma and Louisa into a cab, I went to a random, empty bedroom and fell on the bed. Sammy followed me in, the baby in her arms.

"You are the biggest asshole on the face of the planet," she said as she laid down next to me and put the baby between us.

"Language!" I said, giggling because I thought she was making a joke.

Sammy smacked my arm. "She's wonderful! How can you be so mean to her?"

It took me a moment to realize she was talking about Emma. "I wasn't being mean."

"She's still in love with you."

"Why does everyone think that?"

"I saw how she looked at you. She's barely holding herself together and full of regret. You, meanwhile, ignore her. You're high, drunk, and acting like a teenager."

"I'm coping."

"You told me you were coping by writing this book. Emma told me you wrote it before you even met her. What exactly did you write to cope with Abby?"

"I wrote crap after Abby."

"Are you writing now?" Sammy asked.

"Yes, but it's crap," I said, sitting up, not ready to tell her about this manuscript on my phone. "I can barely function on this tour."

"Maybe if you stayed sober."

"Maybe if Emma went home."

"I am going to keep her in your life. I will call her all the time, invite her to visit, and you will have to see her. You might as well give in to her."

"You can join the Emma Shaw fan club if you want, but you are going to have to fight Patrick to be president."

"Fuck you, Fredrick. I'm going to make you pay for that. Watch me."

She did pay me back. The next night Sammy caught my eye as she placed her adorable baby in the arms of the woman I love. I sat there and watched as the baby fell asleep in Emma's arms. I kept staring at them, and eventually, Emma caught my eye. I could see the tears fill her eyes from where I was sitting. When she looked away, I got up and left. Maybe Patrick and Sammy were right.

"I am not going to Chicago," Patrick said.

"I figured," I said with a shrug.

"You can get through one more city on your own. Seth is coming, and Louisa knows what she has to do. It'll be fine."

"Why is Seth coming?"

"The boy is helplessly in love. Officially, it's so the two of you can work on the TV show scripts together. He doesn't know if Louisa feels the same way."

I didn't have the energy to argue. All I wanted was Emma.

On the plane, Emma told me a story about hearing a couple at the hotel having sex as she and Louisa waited for the elevator. When we were together, Emma was always full of these stories. She has this knack for finding humor in the mundane. I had the sudden urge to fight with her. As we landed in Chicago, I was so full of anger at Emma that I was ready to explode. It came out of nowhere, but it had been pent up for years. I knew that before we left Chicago, we would have a huge fight.

It happened on the second day there. Without Patrick or Louisa to act as a buffer, I just let her have it. I think what set me off happened the day before when Louisa finally asked Emma about the cuppa tea chant. I didn't realize it, but every time Emma chanted it, so did I. I couldn't stop noticing it once she pointed it out. I had taken Emma's habit and made it mine. She was so ingrained in me, and it was infuriating. When she arrived alone to go with me to the signing, I was itching for a fight. Louisa had told me Emma had met with a local publisher while in Los Angeles, a friend of the family. I wondered if Emma was job hunting. I couldn't imagine that she wanted to move to Los Angeles, considering she had refused once before. I assumed she was using this as an opportunity to get more money, especially since she seemed unhappy to be on tour.

I had been obsessing about it since we had arrived in Chicago. Now, as we argued about how unhappy I was, I realized I was standing close enough to kiss her. I wanted to rip off her clothes and throw her on my bed. That is unless she told me to stop, but at that moment, I was positive she wouldn't tell me to stop. I got lost in the fantasy for a moment and lost my chance.

"You want to see a clusterfuck?" she said, taking a step away from me. "I'll give you a clusterfuck. The limo is waiting for you to take you to the bookstore. Feel free to tell them you fired me."

I was alone for the signing. The manager, when I arrived, had a message from Emma. She had already called him.

"I swear, this is her wording, not mine. She said to say it verbatim."

"Ok, I forgive any curse words," I told the manager.

"Get your own fucking cup cup cup cup of tea tea tea tea."

I laughed at the manager.

"She really said that?" I eventually said.

"Yes, can I get you a cup of tea or something else to drink?"

I kept laughing until it was time for me to start the reading. I didn't see her there, but everything ran perfectly as it had for every other event on this tour. She must have been there. I was being immature about this. I was only pushing Emma away when I should have pulled her back in. I should be telling her how wonderful she is, how amazing this tour has been despite my childish behavior, and how wrong I was eight years ago to demand all or nothing. Instead, I continued acting like a child.

It turned out she hadn't left me alone. She had shown up to the event and never said a word.

Emma avoided us the next day, but I knew I needed to apologize for my behavior. If Louisa hadn't insisted on her joining us at Navy Pier, I would have probably given up before I could even start apologizing. If Louisa hadn't been stubborn and just gotten off the wall, she may not have gotten hurt, and I would never have had the courage to try to fix things with Emma. I had never seen Emma so decisive and focused as she was when Louisa fell. Seth and I bickered and tried to figure out how to fix things.

Emma just did it. She called 911, she forbid us from moving Louisa, she rode in the ambulance, called the Musgroves, and talked to the doctors. Emma knew allergies and medical history, so she waited patiently. I found her typing away on her iPad. She made us all type out what we saw happen.

"You are always so calm under pressure," I said to her.

"Someone has to be."

"You knew exactly what to do."

"First aid certification, Girl Scouts, lifeguarding, and my father."

"Why am I not surprised that you are certified for first aid and CPR?" I said.

I watched Emma for a moment. I saw her arms start to shake as the adrenaline wore off.

"I am sorry about what I said yesterday. Considering our history, you've been amazing. Did you call her parents?"

"They should be here soon."

"Seth said he's staying with her. Even if she wakes up, they won't let her fly for a few days. It will be just you and me on the flight back to New York."

"I assumed so. Don't worry, you don't have to talk to me."

My first attempt to fix things had not gone as well as I had hoped. I did learn something about Emma: she had a cross to bear, and she has done it with stoicism since her mother died. I wonder if anyone had ever thanked her or told her she was doing a great job. The next time I tried to fix things with her, I had to approach it differently. I rarely got a chance, though. She slept the whole flight to New York and ditched me as soon as we got to my hotel.

The last leg of the tour was a blur. It felt different without Emma and Louisa. Christi wasn't as organized as Emma was. She did not anticipate needs, which made the last few events in New York City feel frenzied. I shut down and went through the motions. Christi was kind and assumed my disinterest was a mix of physical and emotional exhaustion. She swore most authors experience this even without my tour's drama. I knew she thought the drama was about her injury and Louisa's accident. Nobody knew my past relationship with Emma. Seth kept in touch and passed on messages from Louisa. At night I would lay in bed looking at Emma's contact information. I had her cell phone number and her email address. I used neither, and yet I couldn't delete it. It was all I had left of her. She was gone just as suddenly as she had arrived back in my life.

Seth: Dude, the Musgroves insist you come out to Cape Cod with us.

Fredrick: No - thanks. I'm ready to go home.

Seth: Emma is there.

Seth: Dude, Emma.

Seth: FFS Fredrick

Fredrick: OK

The flight to Cape Cod was filled with Louisa's chatter. You would never know she had been injured a few days ago. She was in love and engaged. Seth was the happiest I had ever seen him. I couldn't help notice the parallels between this and what had happened with Emma eight years ago. They were in the same situation, but with a different result. I was happy for and jealous of Seth. They had found a solution to the problem of geography. They were both willing to change and compromise. It made me more focused on Emma than I had been in the last eight years.

"Daddy, you have to start the BBQ as soon as we get to the house. I want it to be perfect even if Elizabeth Shaw acts like a precious princess diva the entire night," Louisa said to her father.

"Is that Emma's sister?" Seth asked.

"She's the worst," Louisa said. "I love Emma and Mary, but Elizabeth thinks her shit doesn't stink."

"Louisa!" Mrs. Musgrove said.

"Is this not true?" Louisa said to her mother.

"The Shaws have been our best friends for years."

"Exactly, and Elizabeth is the worst. Walter isn't all that much better. I basically like Emma and Mary," Louisa said as she rolled her eyes.

"What does Elizabeth do?" Seth asked.

"Spends her father's money, spends her inheritance, and looks down on everyone," Louisa said.

Seth caught my eye as he tried to get more information from his fiancé. "I mean like, for a job."

"Yes."

"She doesn't work?"

Louisa shook her head. "No, she's a house daughter."

"What the hell is that?" Seth said, laughing.

"Like a housewife, except she is the daughter and doesn't even cook or clean."

"Will I like Mary?" Seth asked.

"She can be very needy, but I think so," Louisa said without thinking long. "Follow Emma's lead because she knows how to deal with her sister. If Emma ignores Mary, then you can too. Never leave Mary out of anything. Plus, my nephews are all types of adorable, but we call them Thing One and Thing Two for a reason. It's total Cat in the Hat chaos with them. They love Emma and me, but they live to torment Elizabeth. You may have to pull them off someone at some point in time. When all else fails, they adore playing on the beach."

"I have made mental notes," Seth said with a smile.

"Plus, Tommy is clearly their father. He is an adult version of them. When I was a baby, I thought his name was monster for the first few years of my life."

"It's true," Mr. Musgrove said without looking up from a book he was reading.

"It's going to be a fun trip, trust me. Ignore snobby behavior, enjoy the food, and play with the kids," Mrs. Musgrove said with a smile.

"I'm sure Emma will be in a much better mood too. She was acting totally weird on the book tour," Louisa said.

"I'm sure she was just exhausted," Seth said, looking at me again.

Tommy was already at the grill when we arrived. He had hotdogs on for his sons, who were precisely as Louisa had told us to expect. They were in the pool with Mary when we got to the house. I think she put so many floaty things on them to immobilize them. Once they were out of the water and on dry land, they were like two pint-size Tasmanian devils.

"Just let them go," Mary said with a sigh as they ran into the house. "They have a whole basement full of toys."

I was talking to Tommy when I saw Emma arrive. As soon as she saw me, she turned around and went back into the house. I could read the panic on her face, even at a distance.

"Well," Seth said, "Louisa was wrong about her being more relaxed."

Seth and I went into the house. In the hour we had been there, he was already comfortable with his future in-laws. They adored him too.

"Where did Emma go? I want to say hi," Seth asked Mrs. Musgrove.

The older woman was standing at the kitchen island, chopping tomatoes and onions for dinner.

"Oh, I suspect down to the basement," the older woman said, wiping her hands on a towel. "Elizabeth, where did your sister go?"

"I am not her keeper. To the moon?" said the other woman in the room.

Elizabeth Shaw looked like Emma, but wrong. Her smile was a sneer, her eyes seemed almost malicious, and she carried herself as if she was better than everyone else. I watched as she poured a glass of wine for herself and failed to offer some to Mrs. Musgrove even though the older woman had an empty glass next to her. Elizabeth just walked out of the kitchen and into the world without caring.

"Nope," Seth said. "She clearly does not realize her shit stinks just as much as everyone's."

Mrs. Musgrove just sighed and shook her head with clear disapproval.

"Try the basement. Emma and those boys are the best of friends," Mrs. Musgrove said before focusing on her prep again.

We found Emma on the floor playing with trucks. I was overcome with emotion as I watched her lay on her stomach and push the trucks around on the floor. I listened to her make motor and siren noises. This should be our life. The two toddler boys looked up and went back to playing. While they may not have reacted to us, our presence changed how one of them played with Emma. He quickly became clingy. He was climbing all over her, and no matter how much she protested, she could not get him off. I felt a new instinct kick in. I have never thought I'm good with kids, but for one moment, I wondered how I would react if these were our children. What if these were our sons annoying his mother? I got up and pulled the boy off Emma.

"Let your aunt take a break. Let's go play on the beach!" I said to him.

Both boys perked up at the idea of playing on the beach. The boy jumped out of my arms and ran out of the room with his brother right behind him. Seth following them, I stayed and helped Emma get up. As she took my hand, I fought the urge to pull her into my arms.

"Thank you," she said.

"My pleasure. All boys have their own way of showing they love you," I said before walking out of the room.

Dinner was more illuminating than it should have been. Even though Seth's official proposal to Louisa was a welcome and happy moment in dinner, I was more interested in two things going on around Emma. I didn't care for Dave. I disliked him when he was flirting with her, but it was what happened at dinner that made me decide I hated him. Even though Dave flirted with Emma, he sat next to Elizabeth at dinner. Periodically, Elizabeth would get up from the table, get a new beer bottle, and sit back down. Then she switched her fresh bottle with Emma's nearly empty bottle. Emma had no idea her older sister was doing this, and Dave said nothing to stop Elizabeth even though he saw the entire thing. He and Elizabeth actually mocked Emma the drunker she got. When I got up to get myself some water, I met Mary by the cooler.

"What is Elizabeth doing to Emma?" I asked Mary.

"I don't know. What is she doing?"

I told Mary what I had seen.

"Fucking Elizabeth," Mary said and searched in the cooler for a bottle of water. "I think she is trying to turn Dave against Emma. Elizabeth and Dave dated until Emma came home after college. When Emma came home, he started paying attention to Emma and ignoring Elizabeth. He has been here flirting with Elizabeth again, so now Elizabeth wants to make sure Emma can't take him away again."

As we sat back down, I watched as Mary exchanged Emma's beer with the bottle of water. She thrust the beer back at Elizabeth but said nothing. When Elizabeth refused to take it, Mary just let it fall into Elizabeth's lap.

The beer spilled and splattered from the bottle covering Elizabeth's dress with beer.

"Fuck you," Elizabeth hissed at her youngest sister.

"No, fuck you," Mary said.

Emma was too drunk to notice any of it but quickly had her own drunken meltdown where she told all of her family off. Everyone was shocked and started talking at once. I watched Emma as she stormed off. I remembered how frank and honest she got when she was drunk. We probably would have danced around our feeling for months if we hadn't gotten drunk together. Now I had my chance to get her to be honest with me. I left the table in time to see Emma leaving the house. I followed her outside and down the street.

"Emma, wait!" I called out when I was close enough.

She stopped and let me catch up.

"You shouldn't walk home alone at night. You could get hit by a car, or who knows what else. Let me walk with you."

"What the fuck do you care for? It's not like I mean anything to you anymore."

"That's not fair. I would feel much better if you let me walk with you. You do realize you're drunk? I mean, you can't even seem to walk right now."

"Whatever."

We walked alone in silence for a while. I tried to decide what I should say next. She stumbled every so often, and I had to take her arm to keep her from falling.

"I decided to come at the last minute. Seth wanted me to come. I should have spoken to you about it first. I'm sorry I just showed up," I said.

"They'll make sure you enjoy yourself."

The way she said it, combined with her reaction at dinner, made me wonder why she kept coming out here every summer.

"Do you not like it out here?" I asked.

"I love it out here. I just happen to not like my family much at the moment."

"Was it this bad when we were at college?"

"I don't remember it being this bad before I left, but I was grieving my mother's death. When I got home, it was like this."

"Dealing with your father is why you are always prepared for a crisis, isn't it?"

"Probably."

"You were amazing in Chicago. I really am sorry I was so nasty to you. Louisa pretty much worships you now that you saved her."

Dave pulled up in a car next to us. Just when I thought I could have a moment alone with Emma, Dave ruined it.

"I thought you could use a ride," Dave said with a look of smug satisfaction.

After the role he played in getting Emma drunk, I was angry that he had the nerve to swoop in to keep her safe. It angered me that she probably was safer in the car with him than walking with me. It angered me that Emma didn't notice the game he was playing. The look on his face, the one that made it clear he knew he was winning, made me want to punch him.

"You are probably safer in the car," I said, leading Emma to the passenger side door and opening it.

"Thank you, Fredrick," she said.

"Emma, come to the fireworks tomorrow night. Promise me you won't punish yourself because you're tired of your father's behavior," I said.

She smiled at me before she closed the door. It was the smile I wanted to see. Maybe Dave wasn't winning? As the car pulled away, I was angry only at myself for having given her up so easily, again.

After that, Dave seemed to be attached to Emma's hip. At the beach the following evening, he was there, by her side and making her laugh. When she moved, he followed her. I was sure she didn't understand what had happened last night and still doesn't know Dave's role in it. It angered me that she seemed to want to be with him.

I am running out of words... Eventually, I will go in and clean this up. That is assuming I want to publish this someday.

It hurts that I know where to find you, what to get you, every little weird thing you do, but I can't kiss you or touch you or even see you smile at me.

I am walking behind you...

I am pretending to do something, but really I am doing this.

Pat's text message exchange while following you around the craft store.

Patrick: Have you gotten laid?

Fredrick: No, you owe me money.

Patrick: I'm flabbergasted. How did you manage to fuck it up?

Fredrick: She met someone else.

Patrick: I refuse to believe it.

Fredrick: His name is Dave and he's a fuck-head.

Patrick: I demand proof.

Fredrick: She's constantly with him.

I stop texting with him at this point because I am watching you. This moment, right now, is the first time I haven't seen Dave attached to your hip.

Patrick: She has been offered an excellent job with a publisher in LA.

Fredrick: She's probably not going to take it.

Patrick: Your friends love her more than they love you.

Fredrick: You aren't helping and I doubt that.

Patrick: She loved you and nobody there knows it... except for Seth.

Lunch -
Ok - so maybe I am wrong about Dave. Preferring a bed of broken glass to spending another night with a person is pretty clear. The thing is, I fear you would say the same thing about spending another night with me.

I can't do this any longer. You have pierced my heart and soul. You are so wrong about everything. You don't see anything. You watched your father grieve the death of your mother for the past fifteen years, and you can't even see my grief over losing you. I have loved nobody but you. Yes, I admit that I have been cruel and resentful, but my love for you has been constant. I came to the Cape for you. All I do is think of you and how much I still want you in my life. Have you not seen this? How can you have misunderstood me?

You are the only person I want a life with, Emma. If that will only happen in New York, so be it. If you have read this far, please end my suffering.

I am half agony, half hope.

Chapter Twenty-Five

I read it three times.

The first time I read it entirely and slowly. I couldn't edit it as soon as I realized what I was reading. By the end, there were so many used tissues next to me that I needed to get another box.

Then I read it the second time. This time I paid attention to moments and things I had missed... Sammy's baby, the benefit at the library, the fight in Chicago, Dave, Elizabeth.

Then I read it a third time and only read the last page...

I am half agony, half hope.

I checked my phone. I had taken more than three hours to read all of the story.

Fredrick: Emma?

Fredrick: Emma?

Fredrick: Emma... did you read it?

Fredrick: Please... say something...

Fredrick: Please text me when you're done reading.

Emma: Where are you?

I didn't get a response, so I tried to think of where he could be. I ran down to the Musgrove's house half a mile away.

"Is Fredrick here?" I said when I got into the kitchen where Mr. Musgrove was making a sandwich. I caught my breath as I waited for his answer.

"He went into town for lunch with Seth and Louisa."

"Thank you," I said and left without waiting for a response.

I started my walk into town and spent the time deciding what to say to Fredrick. I came up with terrible ideas. There was too much to say. I had to explain everything.

I had to apologize. I needed to kiss him. I tried to figure out where they would go for lunch. There were only a few options. I kept checking the time on my phone. Thirty minutes had passed since I had left my house.

I could see the storm beginning to roll in from the west. I was glad I couldn't see the mess my hair must have been because of the humidity. I felt that I needed to find Freddy before the storm hit. I found Seth and Louisa quickly after my long walk.

"Hi!" Louisa said when she saw me. "Why are you all sweaty?"

"Where is Freddy?" I asked and tried to fix my hair and clothes.

"Oh, so you can call him Freddy, but I can't?"

"LOUISA!"

"Interesting," she said, narrowing her eyes. "He isn't here. He was all agitated, so he took the car. He said something about going for a drive. Seth suggested going out to Provincetown."

"What? He's gone?"

"For a while, at least. Want to have lunch with us?"

I didn't respond. I left and started my walk back home.

"Emma, it's about to rain! At least stay with us until it's over!" Louisa called after me.

I didn't care.

Both the rain and my tears held back as I walked home. I was so emotionally exhausted that there was nothing left in me. That all changed when I got to my driveway. The Musgroves' car was there, and Freddy sat on the front step. His long legs were stretched out in front of him and crossed at his ankles. He was leaning back and looking up at the dark clouds above us.

"Freddy?" I said as I walked up the path to the door.

He looked up at me. His eyes were red. In an instant, he was on his feet and walking toward me. I was unable to hold anything back. I ran into his arms and felt them wrap around me as he lifted me up and kissed me. I wrapped my arms around him. I didn't want to pull away. I didn't want to ever be separated from him again. Eventually, we had to breathe, and I heard the rumble of thunder.

"I've been trying to find you since you sent me the text," he said.

"I went to find you. You never responded," I said, opening the front door and pulling him inside with me.

"Emma, I've been responding to you since you sent it."

I pulled out my phone from my pocket and saw I had missed quite a few from many people. I had never turned off the 'do not disturb' option on my phone. I didn't care now and led Fredrick up to my room to be alone.

Chapter Twenty-Six

D o you regret not accepting my proposal?" Freddy asked me as I lay in his arms that night.

"Honestly?" I asked.

"Yes."

I rolled onto my stomach so I could look at him. "Do you think I should have said yes?"

"No," he said after thinking about it for a moment.

I wasn't sure where things stood at the moment. I was ready to accept Ted's job in Los Angeles, but Fredrick was willing to move to New York to be with me. What he didn't know, and I was avoiding, was the formal job offer that Ted emailed me during my father's dinner party. I had already accepted it but hadn't told anyone. It wasn't about Karen's attempts to control my career, my father's needs, or my feelings for Fredrick. I took the job because I wanted it and was excited about Ted's vision for his company.

"I was twenty-two years old, and I was right about my reasons," I said, thinking about my pro and con list. "It's different now, but then, I was right. My regret is just cutting you out of my life as if those two years meant nothing."

Fredrick was silent as it sunk in. "I was angrier at myself than I was with you after a while," he said before brushing my cheek. "I knew you had made the right choice, but I didn't realize it until well after I had accepted what happened. By then, I had already made the movie and assumed you would be suing me. It's not like I fought to keep you in my life. I allowed it to happen, too."

"You were hurt. I understand that."

Fredrick shook his head. "No, we were twenty-two. We lived in a bubble. Your father and Karen made that very clear to me at graduation. Seeing you in your world over the past month made it even clearer. I thought we would just take our Chicago lives, move them to LA, and be happy. Now I know it never could have been that way."

"It's all different now," I whispered.

"Is it?"

"Every reason I had to be here has now become a reason to move to LA."

"Patrick said you were offered a job in LA. Was that what you did while I was there for the tour?"

"Yes, and I accepted it last night. It's a significant raise, enough time off, and telecommuting flexibility so I can be here when needed. It's a chance to use all I have learned and accomplished over the last eight years to my benefit. You're the first person I've told."

Fredrick pulled me closer and kissed me. I knew he wasn't going to argue about this. It was enough for me to know I was important enough to him that he would have come to New York to be with me.

"What about Karen?" Fredrick asked. "Wasn't she a major reason you came back to NYC?"

"She's taken me as far as I can go with her. She has tried to protect and support me but has, unfortunately, only hurt me with the things she did. Like with your book."

Fredrick looked confused.

"She set up email filters without my consent and your manuscript never even made it to my account," I said with a slight frown.

Fredrick grimaced. "My agent was confused when you didn't respond. I even had her send you the manuscript as you had last seen it just to make sure you knew what I wanted."

I tilted my head to the side. "What did you want?"

"Emma, I haven't been angry with you for a long time," he said. "I wanted to see you again and to decide if we could be together again."

"After reading what you sent me, I know. We have a chance to try something different and have a second chance."

"What about Dave?"

I had to laugh. "Did Elizabeth really get me drunk?"

"The last time I saw you that drunk, you climbed onto my lap and kissed me," Fredrick said with a chuckle.

"I didn't feel drunk."

He raised an eyebrow. "You were. What did you think was going on?"

"I'm depressed. I assumed I had just given up, and I liked it."

"Your dad - it's like he woke up when you dared to say no to him. Have you noticed that?"

I had not.

We spent the rest of the night in bed with my bedroom door closed and locked. We only left the room to get food for dinner. We ate in bed and made love over and over. I knew I wasn't going to give him up again. We ignored Elizabeth when she came home, pounded on my door demanding to speak to me, and then jiggled the doorknob trying to break in. We heard my father come up to his room and slam the door shut behind him. I still hadn't taken my phone off 'do not disturb', so I missed phone calls and text messages from Mary and Louisa. Even Freddy put his phone on silent eventually. We weren't ready for the rest of the world. We both wanted to be back in our special bubble, even if only for one night.

Epilogue

A re you excited?" Mary asked me.
    My younger sister and I were sitting in the kitchen
in the home Freddy and I had purchased last September.
His one-room apartment was not the place he wanted to
live anymore. The decision to keep my New York apartment was easy. It meant that I came to LA with nothing
more than my clothes and most important things. Buying
a house together and buying all new furniture was a chance
for us to build a home for both of us rather than trying to
force our old lives on each other. It wasn't large, but it was
ours, it was comfortable, and we loved it. We would use
my apartment in summer to spend a few months there. It
would allow me to see my family and do any East Coast
events.

Freddy proposed with an actual ring and in front of
other people about a month after arriving in LA. This time
there were no lists to help me decide. I said yes immediate-

ly. My father and the Wentworths were all present at the proposal. Freddy had been right about my father changing after my drunken outburst. His anger started a chain reaction that I often wished for. He didn't argue when I told him I was moving to LA and taking a new job. He cried when he took us to the airport. He told me my mother would have been so proud of me. He apologized and started selling his art on his own. He even started freelancing as an editor for new authors and those self-publishing. He had been making money at it, too, and seemed to really enjoy it. I was often reminded that both my parents had taught me the skills that made me good at what I do.

Elizabeth hadn't changed, and I was fine with that. Mary, who took over managing our father's life, was getting some of the attention she had been craving from him. My father was protected financially, which was my priority. The money he made from editing was his money to spend as he wished. If he wanted to give that money to Elizabeth, that was his choice. If Elizabeth felt good about herself and her choices, then I had to butt out. When my father was ready to be more forceful with my older sister, I would back him up.

Elizabeth had been the most upset about my renewed relationship with Freddy, not that she knew that. When Freddy and I finally returned to the world that next morning, she had been waiting for us. She said she had been flirting with Freddy, claiming him. Both Freddy and I were shocked as neither of us had realized any of this. Actually, nobody had realized this. Elizabeth insisted I was only doing this to spite her. We were honest with her, but she turned around and sold the story to tabloids. She remains mad at me. I think she was furious about Dave, who disappeared again after Freddy and I got back together.

Karen had a mixed reaction to my reunion with Freddy. Her real frustration came when I told her I was leaving my job and moving to LA with him.

"After all you have worked for, Emma. You can't give it up now to go to some tiny, LA-based publishing house that is barely surviving," she said.

I had to fight my desire to lash out at her. Since our last conversation about the topic, I had learned what she had done so I wouldn't see Fredrick's emails. I wasn't going to dig deeper since I was committed to moving on without her approval. Still, I was positive I hadn't uncovered all she had done to protect me. Karen was the only one who had tried to support and take care of me in the last decade.

"Karen, I know you think you have been helping me for all these years, but the truth is I think you're hurting my career. I thought I was clear about that already?"

Her jaw dropped. "How so? How have I hurt you?"

I took a deep breath and thought about my words carefully. I was irritated that she pretended that conversation hadn't happened, but I wasn't trying to burn this bridge. "People believed I edited Fredrick's book but passed it on to Christi. Fredrick's agent never heard from me about his book because you broke into my email to delete it. I know you set up filters to ensure I never saw emails from people.

Now agents are writing details into contracts to make sure they work with me and aren't passed off to other editors."

Karen's face got red. "You are working with people who have specifically asked for you. Ted is spreading those rumors to get you to accept this job."

"Karen, these are not rumors. It was something that happened at PubCon."

As she stared at me, something clicked in my head. I leaned back in my chair. "Are you promising agents this so they will sign contracts?"

Karen remained silent and crossed her arms over her chest.

"Once they sign contracts, do you assign them to other editors?" I asked, slowing down my words and hoping she would interrupt to correct me.

"I am preparing you to take over your father's place at the imprint. It's what your mother would have wanted. You need to learn new skills, Emma."

I considered my response carefully. I was angry about her sabotage but using my mother as an excuse hurt. "Karen, I'm not my mother, and I would never have done something because she wanted it."

Karen pursed her lips. "I stand by all the advice I have ever given you."

I pushed my chair away from the table. "Your advice may have been right when I was twenty-two years old. I have the chance to try something new professionally and to have a second chance with the man I've loved for ten years."

"He isn't good enough for you," Karen said as I started to walk away.

I turned back to her. "You know that's not true."

Karen eventually came to terms with my decision to leave the company and the city.

The Musgroves, especially Louisa, were overjoyed that Freddy and I were together. They were also a little annoyed that Seth had known almost everything that was going on and had not told them.

"So, wait," Louisa said. "That means you're Anne in that movie?"

"Yes," I said after a moment. I had never seen enough of the movie to learn the character's name.

Louisa let out an exasperated sigh. "She is nothing like you."

"Some changes were deliberate, and others were seen through a particular filter," Freddy explained as he fought a smile.

"I refuse to believe that character is based on our Emma!" Louisa insisted.

As I promised her in Chicago, I offered Louisa a job in Los Angeles. She hadn't hesitated to accept it. She and Seth were six months away from their own wedding. Her plan to move to LA with Seth meant I would have at least one person from home that I could turn to and increased the chance of family coming out to visit.

I also offered Christi a job in LA, but she passed it up initially. When Freddy reminded her that he was only under contract for one book, she reconsidered and accepted the job. She was already pushing him to write another book for middle school boys. He just signed a new contract with us to publish his next book, with Christi as his editor. He had an idea for another book and claimed Elizabeth was the wicked older sister who inspired it. He was also working on the screenplay for his first book, which there had been a bidding war for the rights to make it into a movie.

He was currently upstairs typing away in his office. I could hear the clack of the keyboard from downstairs. I knew that meant he was excited about what he was working on. There was a secret project that he was keeping from me. He said it was partly what he had written when he had been dealing with the Abby breakup two years ago and partly what he had written while trying to cope with the book tour last year. He and his agent had been in meetings about it, and everyone was keeping their mouths shut. He was going to have to reveal something soon, though. He promised to tell me at the end of the weekend, after the wedding.

I thought about this when my sister asked me if I was excited. How could I not be excited to spend my life doing what made me happy with the man I love?

Preview Pride, Prejudice, and Pledging

Now Available

September

As one of the largest and oldest sororities on campus, there was usually someone in the Phi Alpha Pi two-story Greek revival style mansion. Members were eating, studying, or simply enjoying each other's company. Today there were twenty women moving into their rooms and unpacking for the start of the school year. Lizbeth, as chapter president, had been one of the first sisters to arrive, but still hadn't unpacked. She and the other officers were too busy helping their sisters move in. Lizbeth had already put out a small, literal fire from a fallen candle. Then she put out figurative fires of roommate mix-ups and fights about who got which bed. Now Lizbeth sat alone in her room, exhausted and anxious to get out of the house, if only for a few hours.

Lizbeth had never been this involved in the sorority. She had agreed to the position, for her senior year, to help keep the sorority off academic probation for low grades. This had been a looming threat in the past. Lizbeth had helped by teaching the sorority sisters ways to get organized, creating study schedules, and helping create an atmosphere that turned studying into social events. She was glad her best friend Jane, who was Membership VP, was helping with the move-in. There were sisters that Lizbeth didn't know and relationships she didn't understand. Jane was good at soothing hurt feelings and mediating fights. She had to run a membership meeting later in the day. Rush Week, the week before classes started so potential new members could attend all events, launched tomorrow.

"Lizbeth, did you see the shirts she got the board members?" Marie said, entering her room.

Marie, the sorority treasurer, was holding a hot pink T-shirt up to her body. At twenty years old, she was petite and wore her black hair long with bangs that nearly covered her eyes. When she pulled them back she revealed bright hazel eyes and a nose just a bit too big for her face. Marie was Lizbeth's "little sister," a bond between sorority sisters that often lasted the rest of their lives. As their resident gadget geek, she always had the latest technology toy. She had the first Fitbit, the first GoPro, was also the first to adopt new social media and had happily taken over the sorority's web presence.

Lizbeth had seen the shirt Marie was holding in the gift basket their housemother had given each officer as they moved in. Mrs. C, as they were instructed to call her, was brand new this year and a bit over-eager. She had welcomed each of the officers with a huge hug and said basket, which had also included tons of candy, candles, and school supplies. She gave each sister a candle as she moved in. It was one of these very candles that Lizbeth had put out when it fell and burned the carpet. Their previous housemother had never been this excited to see them.

"Yes, I saw it," Lizbeth said with a sigh.

"Lizbeth, it says, 'It is a truth universally acknowledged, that a single man in possession of a good fortune, must be in want of a wife.'"

"Well, she is up on her Austen," Lizbeth said with a shrug.

Lizbeth sat down on her bed and let herself fall back on the bare mattress.

Marie put her hands on her hips and sighed before responding.

"You know that's not the point. Some of us aren't here to find rich husbands."

"I believe it was the goal for many sisters in her day. She is new and excited. She will learn some of us aren't like this anymore."

"She asked me to wear it tonight."

"No, you'll wear an official sorority shirt; it's tradition."
Marie huffed irritably.

"Are we paying for this stuff? She hasn't handed me receipts, but I'm worried she will."

"Let me know if she does. I think this is her gift to us. She made these herself. I mean, the font is comic sans."

Marie left the room and Lizbeth heard her door bang. All the bedrooms were on the second floor of the house, but the two officer bedrooms were adjacent, so they could all work together. Lizbeth lay back on her bed wishing she wasn't living this close to Marie and her roommate Lydia. She closed her eyes for a few moments, hoping to catch a quick nap.

"I think we have everyone settled and don't need to worry about anything until the meeting starts."

Lizbeth opened her eyes to see Jane come into their room. The only good thing about having to live at the sorority house, as far as Lizbeth was concerned, was rooming with Jane. She had only joined Phi Alpha Pi so she and Jane could be together their freshman year. Last year, when the sorority had just come off academic probation for low grades, Jane and a few graduates had begged Lizzie to run for president. The year had been difficult for some of the sisters, but Lizbeth had emerged as a leader. There was only one other candidate for president: Lydia. Lydia was the de-facto leader of the un-academic sisters and the worst of the lot. In the end, Lydia had taken on the Programming VP role, something she was very good at. Lydia had already planned so many mixers that Lizbeth had forced her to cancel some.

"Is it true there is a party tonight after the meeting?" Lizbeth asked Jane.

"Yes, Lydia planned with the guys at Alpha Pi. They have a few new brothers who transferred from another school and they want to make them feel welcome before Rush Week starts. Do you remember Caroline? Her older brother Charlie is one of those members," Jane added.

Lizbeth nodded, vaguely recalling the woman who had transferred to the university and wanted to get involved at this chapter of Phi Alpha Pi.

"Mrs. C is all abuzz about them because they are so rich."

"Exactly. She thinks Caroline's brother could be a boyfriend for one of us. It is so sweet of her to want to help us."

Lizbeth wished that Jane was being sarcastic, but she knew otherwise. Jane was the kindest person in the world. Jane liked almost everyone, so Lizbeth knew there was something wrong with you if you were the rare person Jane didn't like (and vice versa).

"You're too sweet," Lizbeth said.

"Lizbeth, she's recently widowed. Her children are all off living their own lives. She wants to take care of someone and we need someone looking out for us."

Lizbeth rolled her eyes.

"I understand, and I feel horrible for her. I mean, you saw the shirts. God forbid we learn to take care of ourselves rather than hunt for rich men to marry."

"Some members actually want to meet their future husband. Let her get used to us and learn what we need. I'm sure she'll calm down. If not, well... you'll certainly be a good balance for her. That is one of the strengths we value in you."

Lizbeth tossed a stuffed bear at her best friend before getting up and organizing her half of the room.

Lizbeth watched as Lydia twirled in front of the mirror in the officers' shared bathroom. With bright red hair and green eyes, Lydia was hard to ignore and loved dressing up to get attention. She insisted red-heads had the most fun and made sure to prove it to everyone around her.

"Lizzie, you should totally wear a cute little dress," Lydia said once she stopped spinning long enough to put on her makeup.

"I need my cute little dresses for Rush events. It will just have to be jeans and a shirt," Lizbeth said, pulling her brown hair back in a ponytail.

"At least wear a cute shirt! I can loan you something. I mean, who knows who will be there?"

Lizbeth didn't consider the offer. All of Lydia's shirts were far too tight for Lizbeth's comfort. She was happy to stay in the hot pink sorority shirt she had worn to their earlier meeting.

"It will be the same guys who were there last year and we will outnumber them because most of them aren't back yet," Lizbeth said.

"Caroline's brother will be there! I heard they are filthy rich-- importing and exporting out of New Orleans or something like that. Plus, I heard a friend transferred with him. I know you, Lizzy; once you have a beer or two, you'll be dancing with the rest of us. Maybe one of the new guys will dance with you."

Caroline had been at the earlier meeting and had not impressed her much. As a Phi Alpha Pi member at her previous university, she was entitled to join their chapter without going through Rush week like all new members. Lizbeth hoped Caroline's cold, calculating demeanor was just reserve until she felt more comfortable. Lizbeth seemed to be the only one who didn't like Caroline. She hoped Charlie wasn't anything like his sister.

"Mrs. C thinks Jane and Charlie are perfect for each other," Lydia said as Jane walked into the bathroom.

"When did Mrs. C meet Charlie?" Lizbeth asked.

"He came over with Caroline. You were busy helping people move in," Jane said.

"Did you like him?" Lizbeth asked Jane.

Jane and Lizbeth made eye contact in the mirror.

"I didn't really get to meet him either. I just saw him in passing. Even if he isn't The One, it would be nice to have a boyfriend this year instead of random dates with guys who just want to get laid," Jane said with a small sigh.

"Maybe there will be someone in your classes," Marie said from outside the bathroom.

"I'm an education major, Marie. Most of the guys in my classes are gay or married," Jane said.

Some of the residential sisters walked to the Alpha Pi house together. Lizbeth enjoyed the company of her sorority sisters in small amounts, like this brief walk, and before they started drinking. Lydia was completely unpredictable once she started drinking, oscillating between mean girl and sweet angel. Then there was Marie, who had offered to be sober sister before they left the house. Others were with them, but having their own conversations as they walked.

"My parents were in China most of the summer, so I had the house to myself. I had a ton of pool parties," Lydia said as they walked.

"I spent the summer in L.A. with a cousin who is making YouTube videos out there. I got to hang out at the Nerdist offices a couple of times," Marie said.

They could hear the music playing at the house as they got closer. The Alpha Pi house was one of three fraternity houses on this street. The other two had lights on but were quiet. The fraternities didn't take Rush Week as seriously as the sororities did. The members would show up on campus tomorrow, open the doors and potential members would just come around. The sororities had constant events: teas, meet & greets, dinners, ceremonies, and more. Tonight, anyone from the fraternities was probably hanging out at the Alpha Pi house because there was nothing else to do. There were so few guys on campus that the Phi Alpha Pi sisters would still outnumber them easily.

The party had started on the lawn of the fraternity house but was pretty tame so far. Guys were just hanging around. Other women were there, mostly girlfriends. Most of the other sororities were deep into Rush Week prep. Lydia and Jane had assured Lizbeth everything was done for their opening tea. Lizbeth suspected Lydia had suckered Mrs. C into helping set up while they partied.

The group of sisters had split up once they got to the lawn. Lydia had a beer in hand and was on the back of some fraternity brother, riding him around the lawn before the other sisters got into the house. Lizbeth ended up with her friend Charlotte, who met them at the party. Jane and Lizbeth had known each other as children, having spent summers at the same sleep-away camp. Charlotte had been one of their suite-mates their freshman year. Lizbeth, Charlotte, and Jane had all joined the sorority to be able to hang out together. Charlotte was nowhere near as involved as Lizbeth and Jane. She only did the minimal activity to stay active. This meant coming to weekly meetings at the house and the occasional event. Charlotte was tall and lanky with skin the color of milk chocolate. Her big brown eyes dominated her face and she wore her curly black hair cut close to her head, making her look mature and sophisticated. Charlotte, a painter, frequently looked like she had just come from her studio. Lizbeth could see the paint splattered on her jeans.

"It looks like Jane has a new friend," Charlotte said as she and Lizbeth sat down on a bench on the back deck of the fraternity house.

"That's Caroline, who just transferred here with her brother. She was at the meeting earlier."

When Lizbeth looked at Caroline she thought of southern women from the 60s. Caroline was tall and rail-thin with long blond hair that had dark roots. Her almond-shaped hazel eyes gave her an exotic look. Lizbeth wondered if Caroline had done a small amount of plastic surgery --especially her too straight nose. She had been in clean jeans and a white blouse at the earlier meeting, but now she had changed into an A-line black skirt and put a black cardigan over the blouse. She also wore two-inch black wedges that made her tower over most of the other women in the room.

"I must have missed her," Charlotte said. "Is her brother the cute blond guy talking to them?"

Lizbeth looked back at the two men standing with Caroline and Jane. Caroline was wearing an expression that Lizbeth's younger sister Becca (her biological sister) called resting bitch face. Lizbeth suspected this was her default expression. One of the two guys looked like Caroline and could only be her brother, Charlie. After all the fuss Mrs. C had been making, Lizbeth expected Charlie to be some golden Adonis. He was cute, but not Lizbeth's type. He had a huge, dopey grin on his face, and was staring at Jane like a puppy dog. His hair was straight, blond, and worn longer in the front than the back. He had a tall, athletic, stocky build, and was wearing distressed jean shorts, a grey T-shirt, and flip flops. The other man was the same height as Charlie but had a slender build. He stood very straight and very still. His expression was a mix of annoyance and boredom. Lizbeth thought he would have been cute if it wasn't for the sour expression. He had dark brown hair that curled just a little at the edges as if it was ready for a quick trim. He was wearing dark jeans and a black button-down shirt. He had rolled up the sleeves of the shirt because of the heat. Lizbeth noticed he was wearing maroon Chucks on his feet.

"I assume that's Caroline's brother since they look so much alike. I don't know who the other guy is, though," Lizbeth said.

"His name is Wil and he is super-duper rich," Lydia said, coming out of nowhere and dropping down on the bench between Lizbeth and Charlotte.

"Is he the other transfer?" Charlotte asked.

"Yep, he is some orphan from New York. His family was like huge in real estate. Like Trump-huge. They have oodles of money. He might be richer than Caroline and Charlie. He's a pill though. He won't talk to anyone except Charlie and Caroline. You have to meet them, Lizzie!" Lydia said and pulled Lizbeth to her feet.

"Hi!" Jane said with a smile as they approached the group. "This is Charlie and Wil. They're the new Alpha Pi brothers who just transferred here. Charlie is Caroline's brother. Lizbeth is our sorority president and my best friend. Charlotte is our former roommate and a sorority sister."

"It's really nice to meet you," Charlie said to the pair.

Charlie had an easy smile and was clearly used to enjoying himself. Wil, on the other hand, looked incapable of smiling. His lips were thin and Lizbeth wondered what he would look like if he just smiled a little. Now that she was close enough she could see that his eyes were green with dark rings around the iris. She found herself drawn to his eyes, glancing back at him to look into them again.

"It's great to meet you too," Lizbeth said to Charlie. "Welcome to campus. Are you living at the house?"

"No," Charlie said. "The three of us are sharing a town-house just off-campus. Our parents didn't want us to worry about dorms and felt more comfortable with Wil as our roommate."

"Did you all grow up together? I thought someone said you were from New Orleans. Jane is from New Orleans, too," Lydia asked.

"We're from New Orleans. Wil and I have been friends for years. Our mothers went to college together. We all wanted to keep the tradition going, even as far as transferring schools together. Wil's family is from New York, though," Charlie said.

"Lizzy has family in New York!" Lydia said.

"In the city?" Caroline asked.

"Yes. My father's parents live there. We visit them a few times a year."

"Where does your family live?" Charlie asked.

"Boston. My mother's family has lived in Boston since the pilgrims. They still live on the out in Central Massachusetts on the family farm."

"Boston is a long way from Georgia," Caroline said.

"It was in the middle between Jane and me. We wanted to go to college together, so we picked middle ground. It's a long way from New Orleans too," Lizbeth said.

"It is twice as far from Boston to Atlanta than it is from New Orleans," Wil said.

"Yes, I'm aware," Lizbeth said.

"Then it's not equal distance nor is it middle ground."

Lizbeth looked at Wil with narrowed eyes.

"It was affordable for both of us compared to other options," Lizbeth said.

Wil didn't respond and the conversation turned to great bars and restaurants around the campus. Lydia took over and dominated the conversation. Charlie periodically asked Jane questions that Lydia answered. Wil just stared at Lizbeth for the rest of the conversation.

"I'm going to find another beer," Lizbeth said, the empty bottle her excuse to walk away.

Charlotte followed her with a wave to the others. By the end of the night, the pair was tipsy and giggling on the floor of the fraternity game room under the pool table. They were both tired of talking to the same drunk guys for the past three years and had been reduced to mocking those guys in whispers even though they were alone in the room.

"His lisp gets worse when he drinks. Why does he torture himself?" Charlotte said about one of the sophomore brothers who often hit on Lizbeth.

"Shhh," Lizbeth said when she heard the game room door open and two people walk in.

"I like this group better than the brothers at Tulane," one voice said.

"Yes, well, it is nice to have an actual house to hang out at. This group certainly has a better standing on campus and will yield better connections for the future," the other replied.

The two pairs of legs stopped right next to the pool table. Lizbeth recognized the maroon Chucks. The two men could only be Charlie and Wil. Lizbeth heard billiard balls being knocked around above them.

"The Phi Alpha Pi sisters seem friendly. Jane's very pretty," Charlie said.

"She was very accommodating and sweet. She smiles a lot, but so do you."

"Lizbeth is also very pretty."

"Yes, but not my type. You know me and sorority girls. I don't enjoy women who drink themselves stupid when they aren't aggressively trying to attract wealthy men so they can elevate themselves socially and financially. The Phi Alpha Pi chapter here doesn't have the best reputation. Caroline considered not joining the chapter."

Lizbeth could feel her face flush. Charlotte grabbed her arm and covered her mouth to keep Lizbeth from revealing their location. They waited until Charlie and Wil ended their conversation and left the room.

"I'm too aggressive? I'm drinking myself stupid? I'm trying to elevate myself financially and socially?" Lizbeth said when they were alone again.

"Calm down. Don't let the opinion of one unpleasant man upset you. He clearly knows nothing about you."

"He judged me based on one twenty-minute conversation, and the entire sorority on rumors!"

"Come on, let's get out of here. It's not like you have to deal with him. How often do we party with the fraternity?"

"All the time, Charlotte! We have parties with them all the time," Lizbeth said, her voice rising.

Charlotte dragged Lizbeth from the room and forced her to walk through the house to make sure all the sisters were safe. They found Marie taking her sober sister duties very seriously and decided to head back to the house on their own. They were about halfway down the block when Lydia ran up behind them.

"Charlie and Caroline are totally going to host a Halloween party at their townhouse!" Lydia yelled as she caught up with Lizbeth and Charlotte.

"Really?" Lizbeth said.

"Yep! Charlie promised they would host a party."

"Wait, did he say a Halloween party or did you decide that?" Charlotte asked.

"He said they would have a party. I suggested Halloween and nobody said no."

Get *Pride, Prejudice, and Pledging* to read more!

Do You Want A Little More?

Modern Persuasion may be over but the stories don't end there!

A Little More Modern Persuasion is a collection of short stories that connect Modern Persuasion to the other books in the 21st Century Austen series.

Grab your copy of A Little More Modern Persuasion from Amazon or get a preview of the stories by downloading "Emma's Hour" (https://dl.bookfunnel.com/qx9xfd x74i).

Reader's Guide

1. Modern Persuasion is a modernization of Jane Austen's Persuasion. What similarities did you notice between the two novels? What differences?

2. Who would you cast for each of the characters in a potential movie version of Modern Persuasion?

3. Emma, at 22, makes the decision to end her relationship with Fredrick in order to pursue her own goals and dreams. What would you have done in her place?

4. Emma realizes, years later, that while she made the right decision, she saw it as all or nothing instead of trying to find a solution that made them both happy. What options do you think the two of them ignored?

5. Is there a decision you have struggled to make, made the best choice with the information you had, but regretted the decision later?

6. What is the hardest decision you have had to make in your life, so far?

7. When reading Fredrick's section, it becomes clear that both Fredrick and Emma misinterpret each other's expressions, body language, and even words. How often, in your opinion, does this make situations go bad or get worse?

Do you have a book club that wants to read Modern Persuasion?
Sara is happy to visit your book club virtually or, when possible, in person. We can also provide copies of the book if needed.

Learn more on the 21st Century Austen Book Club page.

http://saramarks.net/book-club-support/

Ready to be More Than A Reader?

I love my readers, especially those who read all the books and share their thoughts. There are some readers who want to be more – they want to be collaborators!

Are you ready to be a collaborator? If so, join me on Patreon as we work to get the next books ready for publishing! The current project for the Rom Com/Women's Fiction collaborators are working on Unravelling Carrie Woodhouse, the next book in the 21st Century Austen series, and the related short story collection. It's another Emma modernization that will probably be published in May 2022.

How does it work?

For $2.00 a month you get to read chapters as they are edited and written. The next year, when the book is published, you get an autographed copy with your name listed as a collaborator in the front of the book.

In addition, you get swag, to preview book covers, give feedback on the release plan, and read all the short stories.

Does this interest you? If so...

Join me on Patreon!

https://www.patreon.com/saramarks

Acknowledgments

When I started writing as part of National Novel Writing Month, I was sure that almost everything I ever wrote would be pure trash. So much to that I printed a copy of said trash and put it on my bookshelf. For me, I was simply proud that I had put on paper all these ideas that had been swirling in my head for years. I added, instead of a dedication, instructions for what to do with these upon my death: read highlighted passages at my funeral so everyone can have a good laugh. I still give my family and friends permission to do that, but hopefully this book will provide a different kind of tribute.

Writing this book was a labor of love. Persuasion is my favorite of Austen's novels. It took three years to go from idea to final product and was one of the most rewarding experiences of my life. There are many people to thank, some of whom I can acknowledge and some I can't.

First, to Jane Austen, who provided the first inspiration and wrote the original.

Second, to Christi, who always liked every draft of this novel even when she hated my choices on which characters to remove. You helped give me the courage to publish it.

To Laura and Barbara, you both did an amazing job helping me edit. I don't think this would have been ready without both of you! Barbara, I had to keep a lot of the curse words in. Patrick wouldn't have been the same without them.

To Frank, Etta, and Sande who did grammatical spot-checking.

To the organizers of National Novel Writing Month, who put together a program that motivated me to start writing the things in my head. This novel was a product of the July 2014 Camp NaNoWriMo program.

To the members of the Friendly Book Club, my favorite book club, thank you for helping me construct the reader's guide so that other groups like us can have conversations like ours!

Finally, to the authors of SIPA and NaNoLowell who have led me by example and continue to inspire.

About Sara

After a mid-life crisis and failing out of college at the age of twenty, Sara Marks decided to live the life she wanted, not the one expected of her. Now a librarian with two master's degrees, she plans to never stop getting over educated. She started writing as part of the National Novel Writing Month program over fifteen years ago. She likes to write about confident women who deal with classic problems. Sara's a hopeless romantic who is unlucky in love. She cries at nearly every movie she sees (ask her about when she cried at a horror movie), but it's full-on weeping for Disney animated movies. She likes her caffeine cold and her alcohol bubbly.

Find Sara on these social media platforms:

Facebook: https://www.facebook.com/saramarks01

Instagram: https://www.instagram.com/lifeplantser/

GoodReads: https://www.goodreads.com/author/show/15507164.Sara_Marks

Patreon: https://www.patreon.com/saramarks